Pieces in Time

Pieces in Time

AN ADVENTURE BY

DANIEL R. M. GILBERT

Gilbert Books

Simpsonville, South Carolina

2014

To my wife,
Emilie

and our three munchkins
Miles, Seth, and
Bethany

Contents

Acknowledgments

This novel was a long time in the making...5 years. It started as a simple line on a computer screen during a long and sleepless night.

To George, Donnie, Randy, and everyone else who walked by that computer, thanks for being my sounding board.

To Todd and Jimmy, thanks for your input and begging for more when I would drag my feet and leave the character hanging.

To Robyn, I can't thank you enough for all the editorial work you have put into this book and for the cover art.

Josh, the title was your idea and it beat all the other suggestions hands down.

And last but not least, to my wonderful wife Emilie, without you this book would have never been. Your ideas, plot twists, and the insistence on "Aha!" moments made this book what it is.

Thank you all for your support.

Prologue

Darkness…helpless, hopeless, friendless, and fruitless; the early years of one's life can be truly desolate when you face them alone…

"That is a seriously depressing way to start your memoirs, Sir." Martin Smith appeared to be in his late seventies. He had a British accent that seemed to fit with his stiff demeanor and dry sense of humor. He was currently dusting off various books and trinkets on the wall of shelves behind his employer. It was an impressive collection of antiques from all over the world, and Martin had decided to clean them as much as possible whenever Mr. Jonson was trying to write his memoirs. They were never that dirty, they were just a convenient excuse for Martin to read over Mr. Jonson's shoulder. It wasn't because he wanted to write the book himself, Martin had every confidence that Mr. Jonson knew his own life story, he was only there so that he could offer his counsel if needed and to make sure his boss didn't stretch the truth too much.

David Jonson was old. His hair had long since turned snowy white but thankfully had never thinned out. His bluish-gray eyes danced as he looked around his spacious office, amazed at what he had accomplished in his long lifetime. He let his eyes linger on the twelfth century Chinese fan hanging over the sofa, hoping to receive some sort of inspiration. Failing to rouse the muse, he looked at Martin and sighed.

"Martin, the first few years of my adult life were filled with failure and disaster. I can't think of any other way to start my memoirs and still be truthful." Exasperated, he sat at his desk staring at the computer monitor. He had been trying to start his autobiography for about a week, but every time he thought he was making progress his assistant would ridicule his work and he would start over. The more he thought about it, the more he realized that Martin wasn't going to leave him alone until he got it just right. He eyed his assistant suspiciously. "So, how would you start the story of my life if you were writing it?" Martin replaced a solid gold statue of an eagle he had been polishing, joined his boss behind the large oak desk in the center of the room, and prepared to give him some much needed advice.

"If I were you, I would start with something along the lines of, 'Back in my day,' or, 'When I was a young man.' I would not start with something that is going to make the reader think that the only reason you wrote your book was just to complain about the world. It needs to be an attractive beginning, not a depressing abhorrence of your prior circumstances to the extent that your readers think you were suicidal. If you feel compelled to crush the heart and soul of your readers, you should at least wait until the end of the book to drop the bad news on them. That way they would have had the book long enough that they would not be able to return it, and you would not lose any money on refunds. Besides, all of your supposedly wrong choices and big mistakes eventually led you to the biggest adventure anyone could ever hope for."

"Martin, as old as I am, I won't have to worry about giving any refunds. But, since you seem so determined to give me your two cents' worth, and you want it to be more 'attractive'…" Mr. Jonson cleared the text from his screen, paused for a moment, then began to type a new opening for his book.

So there I was, 30,000 feet, inverted, with a sling-load. It was up to me to save the aircraft and the cargo from complete destruction. One engine was trailing smoke and the other had stopped working three hours ago. The pilot had abandoned the aircraft when we encountered the first flight of MIGs, and the copilot had gone completely insane after the third. If our mission failed, hundreds of Indonesian cats would starve to death. Thinking fast, I pulled out my trusty nine millimeter sidearm and–

Martin cleared his throat. "I said 'an attractive beginning' not a convoluted fabrication. That beginning is so wildly unbelievable that nobody would even make it through the checkout line with that book, let alone want to read the whole thing." He started ticking off points with his fingers, "First of all, the only type of aircraft that can carry a load externally on a sling is a helicopter, and those do not go much higher than 10,000 feet. Second, if you did manage to get inverted with a sling-load it would come crashing down and destroy the aircraft. Third, an aircraft, even without a sling-load, does not remain airborne for three hours after losing an engine, especially with the other engine smoking. Fourth, a trained pilot would never jump out of an aircraft he was in control of. Fifth, one MIG could take out a lone helicopter from far enough away that you would not have known he was there. Six …"

"Okay, point taken." Jonson's eyes fixated upon his keyboard. "I am trying to make the book a real page burner. People want action and adventure. Who cares if it is all made up or blown out of proportion?"

"With all due respect, that beginning sounds like the excerpt on the back of a B movie you might find on the discount rack at the local supermarket."

Looking up from his keyboard Jonson asked, "That bad, huh?"

"Yes, Sir."

Mr. Jonson scratched his head and thought for a moment. He really did want the opinion of his assistant or he would have just locked himself in his room and given orders not to be disturbed. As a matter of fact, Martin was his most trusted companion. The fact that he was considered an employee never had any ill effects on the friendship that had formed over the years. If anything, it helped to make it grow stronger.

"All right, Martin, I'll bite. How would you begin to write my memoirs?" Jonson slid the keyboard over to his butler. A small smile worked its way across his lips. If Martin was determined to have his say in the matter, he might as well help.

"Well, Sir, I would probably start something like this...."

Once upon a time...

Jonson cleared his throat. "Do I look like fairy tale material to you?"

Martin shook his head no.

Jonson continued, "Then I suggest you try something a little bit different."

"As you wish."

In the beginning God created–

"Martin, I'm not *that* old, and I think that opening has been taken. Not to say that it was a bad opening, it's just that I don't think my memoirs are going to be quite that caliber."

"Perhaps you are correct, Sir. How about this...."

Chapter 1
The Beginning of My Story

It was the turn of the millennium. I had just graduated from high school and was trying my best to find my place in the world. However, discovering my niche was not as easy as it might have seemed in the small town of Buck Hill Falls, Pennsylvania.

My first job was innocent enough, a paper route. Now don't get me wrong, I loved my paper route. After tightly binding each of the papers, I would place them in the passenger seat of my two-seater sports coupe and commence delivery, bright and early every day.

Okay, maybe I didn't get the papers delivered as early as I was supposed to; at eighteen years old, noon was bright and early to me. Also, I didn't exactly use the highest quality rubber bands to hold the papers together, so some of them inevitably came apart when I threw them. And if by chance they didn't come apart in flight, they came apart on impact. But being persistent, I managed to get most of the papers to their rightful subscribers on the proper days. Unfortunately, there were the few times that I ran late and tried to set the world land speed record on my route. Speed did not help my accuracy as I tossed the papers. Total damage included three broken living room windows, a topless bird bath, and a headless garden gnome, along with two speeding tickets for driving in excess of twenty over the limit.

"You know, Martin, in retrospect, I must admit that I was purposely aiming for that garden gnome, but the other stuff was purely accidental."

"Of course you were, Sir. However, I do not believe

that your readers need to know about your gnome-icidal
tendencies."

Three weeks into my first job I was in the hole $2,000,
and was close to losing my driver's license. Needless to say I
didn't last long as a paper boy.

My second job was a little bit better than my first,
primarily because I lost less of my own money. I had decided
to try valet parking at an upscale restaurant on Main Street.
For the first four months I did well. I managed to make just
enough money to pay back all of the people I owed for their
broken windows and even got my tickets paid down. And
then–

"Martin, do we have to tell them about the Camaro?"
"Yes. I believe that by telling your readers about your
faults, it shows that you are not perfect. It makes you easier
to connect with in the reader's mind."
"If you say so, just tell me when it's over."

It was a 1968 Chevrolet Camaro SS, midnight blue with
white racing stripes. It was love at first sight as the car pulled
up to the restaurant's valet parking area.

The driver stepped out of the car, walked to the
passenger's side, and opened the door for his date. A
gorgeous woman–blonde, five-foot-four, and one hundred
fifteen pounds–stepped out of the car and did a double take
when she saw me. Her date took her by the arm and said to
her, "Come on, Susan, we are going to be late." He turned to
me and handed me the keys and said, "Not a scratch."

I nodded, handed him his ticket, slid into the driver's
seat, and started the engine.

The car's leather interior had that just-rolled-off-the-
assembly-line smell, and its engine sounded like distant

thunder. The vibrations coursing through the car gave me a feeling of power that I immediately fell in love with.

Completely overwhelmed with pure elation, I quickly pulled away from the entrance of the restaurant. Unfortunately, the Camaro's passenger door was still open and scraped against the awning support column before slamming shut. My face turn a putrid shade of pale yellow, and a nauseating feeling manifested itself in my gut.

Panicking, I leaped out of the car to survey the damage. The car lurched forward, knocked me to the pavement, and started rolling down the street. Only then did I realize that I had forgotten to take the car out of gear.

Have you ever had that feeling that as bad as it might seem, it's just going to get worse? Well, it did.

I jumped up from the ground and gave chase to the car. The car was traveling downhill and quickly picked up speed. Even though I was giving it my best effort, soon the car was traveling too fast for me to catch on foot and all I could do was watch and feel that sickening sensation in my stomach grow more and more prominent. I prayed that the car would run off the side of the road and hit a nice soft trash mound or even a bush.

Unfortunately, the Camaro had a mind of its own. It kept to the center of the road better than most drivers do on the way to church, even managing to miss all of the potholes in the street. By the time it reached the first intersection, the Camaro was traveling twenty-five miles per hour. Luckily, there was nobody at that intersection, but that luck didn't hold out for long.

The Camaro and the city's number six ladder truck reached the next intersection, 21st and Main, at the exact same time. The fire truck didn't even slow down. The sound of the crash was horrendous–crashing, mashing metal screeching in pain. Everyone in the restaurant came running out to see what had happened. With every flip of the car, my stomach rolled. The Camaro was so mangled that it took the fire fighters forty-five minutes to determine that there was nobody in the car then another ten to figure out where it had come from.

The damage was so extensive that the man who had trusted me with the car didn't even recognize it until I handed him the license plate. As the man read the plate's numbers, AXE 248, a variety of emotions flashed across his face–confusion, disbelief, anger, and finally shock that the car he had driven to the restaurant was now in a thousand different pieces strewn across the road. Then suddenly a peaceful look fell upon his face, his eyes rolled back in his head, and he promptly collapsed onto the ground.

My guardian angel must have been watching over me that night, because I was not held accountable for the replacement costs. Later I learned that the car didn't belong to the driver, it belonged to his girlfriend's boss, who had asked her to pick it up from the paint shop. The car's owner insisted that the man who had borrowed the vehicle pay for it, and thankfully, didn't hold me or the restaurant responsible. However, I was fired anyway and black-listed from every restaurant in town.

After ruining any chance at working at a restaurant again, I took a job as a–

"Martin, if you know what's good for you, you will skip the job with me in a chicken suit."

"But, I believe that your failed attempt in the advertising business and the resulting demolition of the Gomez brand chicken processing plant would help the reader to recognize your early propensity toward failure and destruction that if left unchecked would have cause your life to spiral–"

"Just leave it out of the book for now. I'm sure you will find some way to work it in later."

"As you wish."

The inspiration for my next avenue of employment presented itself in the form of a flier. It was a picture of an old man in a funny suit with a ridiculous hat and a caption that read, "Uncle Sam wants YOU for the U.S. ARMY!" Having grown tired of breaking things and getting fired, I decided to visit my local recruiter. I didn't realize what I was getting myself into but thought at the time that it had to be better than my other jobs.

As you read this memoir, there are things you need to be aware of. Number One: Recruiters lie. It doesn't matter if they are recruiting for Avon, Amway, or the Army, they always bend the truth into a pretzel. Recruiters expound upon the perks, such as travel opportunities, college money, and easy advancement, while neglecting to mention the drawbacks–berating, intimidation, hostile fire, and annual dues. Number Two: Recruiters are on commission. They get bonuses based on the number of people they sign up, regardless of their abilities. Number Three: Recruiters are smooth talkers. Being naive, I had happily signed away the next eight years of my life to explore the world and meet new people, not realizing that sometimes the new people I would meet would try to kill me.

In anticipation of starting my new career, I prepared myself mentality by watching my favorite military movie and made myself participate in a rigorous physical fitness program. By the time I left for basic training, I could quote the movie, word for word, and make it to the refrigerator and back faster than Private Leonard Lawrence could fire his two shots. I thought I was ready for anything. Boy was I wrong.

My orders were to report to Fort Jackson in Columbia, South Carolina, on the eighth day of August. It was the hottest summer on record, and it didn't help that Jackson was located in the bottom of a valley that had no air flow. During my first month on base, the temperature and the humidity stayed in the high nineties, and the air rarely moved. I quickly learned why it was called the armpit of the south.

Two words best describe basic training: culture shock. There were hundreds of people on base with every race, color, and creed packed into sixty-man bays. There was no personal space, and privacy is something that you learn to do without. But the worst part was the irate man with sergeant stripes on his collar and a large brown hat on his head, lovingly referred to as "Drill Sergeant," who followed you around and yelled twenty-four hours a day.

The first part of basic training is reception. Day one of reception consisted of the most invasive physical exam I have ever endured. I was asked my name, birth date, and social security number and told to wait in line. The first stop was the legal center. This is where I had to sign my life away for the next eight years to Uncle Sam without hope of parole or reprieve. I spent an hour and a half waiting in line to sit with a lawyer for ten minutes of required questions ranging from, "Do you have any felonies on your record or currently pending with the court?" to, "Do you have a history of domestic violence?" After all the questions about my past, I had to sign a document that stated that I would not sue the U.S. Army for any harm that came to me during training due to carelessness on my part, whether it was mental or physical. It was explained to me later that if I was injured during training, it was automatically considered carelessness on my part. When I had scribed my John Hancock on all the required documents, it was back to standing in line.

The second station was the barber. As with normal, civilian barbers, you sit down in the chair, they ask you your preference of hair style, and then begin to cut your hair.

That's where the similarities cease. By the time I realized they weren't just taking a little off the top, I was completely bald. And, to add insult to injury, the Army had made me pay three dollars for the service. The only thing that helped console me for the loss of my dignity was that everyone in the room, except the barbers, had the same hair style. It was the same story with everyone that went in there, "Sit down, Sir," "How are you, Sir?" or "How would you like your hair, Sir?" and then, zip zip buzz buzz, all their hair was gone and the Drill Sergeant was screaming at them to move to the next station.

After the barber, we were all herded into a large room and told to wait until we were called. This is when I learned the unofficial Army motto of "hurry up and wait." While waiting to be called into the next room, I began to realize that I was no longer a civilian. But I wasn't quite a soldier either. I couldn't put my finger on the correct terminology, but I knew I didn't qualify as either of those two classes of people. I soon figured out what I was when several of my companions and I were corralled into a large examination room, told to quickly and quietly remove all clothing, except for our underwear, and to line up facing the door with our toes on the tape. We were cattle. Grade A, number one, USDA choice beef.

As the doctors began to circle us and take their notes, a chuckle started to spread throughout the room. Everyone had reached the same conclusion that I had, and a singular thought went through all of our heads at the same time. *MOO*. The doctors then began running us through a series of motions in order to determine our level of fitness. Having been training for several days before I arrived, I was surprised when the doctor who examined me just shook his head and muttered in disgust. He handed me a cup, a lid and a label, told me not to drip, and sent me to the bathroom.

Upon my return, I was told to get dressed and resume my place in line.

The next station was blood draw. The nurse had me sit down in a small chair that looked like a cross between a middle school chair, complete with desk, and a medieval torture device. She strapped my right arm down and set three large vials on the table. Then she pulled out a syringe that looked like it had a ten penny nail attached where the needle was supposed to be. I started having a familiar sensation in my gut as thoughts of a blue and white sports car filled my mind.

The last stop in my long and invasive tour of the in processing building was immunizations. After an hour-long search for a vein in my arm, I didn't think it could get much worse. Once again I was amazed at my ability to be mistaken. The drill sergeants had us all line up single file and take one step at a time through a huge room lined with medic trainees. Step… step… stick! Step… step… stick! Every two steps brought a new sensation into my arm. The first shot just burned a little. The second made my arm a little sore. After the fourth shot, I had no feeling from my shoulder down. By the end of the line, I had had a total of eight shots, four in each arm, and I was feeling fairly sick to my stomach. The only thing that had kept me going through the immunization process was the promise of going to bed soon thereafter. Unfortunately, the drill sergeants had to have one more laugh at our expense; they took us to the chow hall for dinner.

The day after I received the stamp of approval, I was assigned to a holding platoon until a training spot opened up. During this period of voluntary incarceration, I met with some trainees who were, at least in my opinion, destined to receive the Darwin Award. One such individual would take any bet or dare that involved money. Some bets were harmless enough, such as, "I bet you can't do one hundred push-ups in a two-minute period" or, "I bet you can't outrun me in a two mile run." Others were a bit more senseless, and therefore more dangerous. These would include things like, "I dare you to run down to the drill sergeant's office and pound on the door wearing nothing but your skivvies," or "I dare you to dive off the top bunk onto the mattress on the floor." When our resident simpleton, also known as Private Cameron, tried the dare with the drill sergeant's door, the entire platoon wound up in the grass doing push-ups, sit-ups, and mountain-climbers until dawn. After that episode, we decided to limit the bets and dares to things that would only affect the individual who accepted them.

One week after that long night in the grass, the most menacing and subsequently the most imbecilic dare was issued to Private Cameron. One of our platoon mates had brought along a tube of Icy Hot and thought it would be absolutely hilarious if someone were to rub a handful all over their groin area. Of course, Cameron couldn't turn down such a challenge, especially when he was offered twenty dollars to accomplish the feat. The private, having demanded "Show me the money," squeezed out a large handful of the white cream and eased his heavily medicated hand down the front of his shorts. At first there was no reaction. Then, very slowly, we began to see a bead of sweat form on his forehead and trickle down his nose. It was at this precise moment that the drill sergeant decided to make a surprise inspection of the barracks. As soon as he stepped into the room, we all went to parade rest and stood silently, waiting for instructions. That is, everyone except Cameron. As the drill sergeant walked down the row of bunk beds, we heard Cameron start to breath heavily. When the drill sergeant had walked half way down the row, Cameron started to whimper. By the time he reached our distressed colleague, Cameron was soaked with sweat and making the most awful moaning noises I had ever heard.

The drill sergeant sniffed the air, recognized the smell and chuckled to himself. We heard him mutter something about one in every cycle and watched as he left the room. As soon as Cameron was sure the drill sergeant was gone, he ran into the latrine and locked the door.

There is something that should be known about Icy Hot before I continue. One of its active ingredients is methyl salicylate. It is the substance that reacts with the water on your skin to create that warming sensation. More water equals more heat.

As we stood outside the latrine, we could hear Cameron as he stripped off his clothes and turned on the shower. As much as we thought he deserved it for doing it in the first place, we did try to stop him from getting into the shower. When we had finally managed to get the door open, the damage had already been done. Private Cameron was screaming like a school girl and lying on the shower floor. He had chemical burns from his belly button down to about mid thigh. The drill sergeant, having known what was going on just by the smell and the look on that private's face, had already made the proper phone calls and arrived with the medics soon thereafter. We never dared anyone to do anything else after that.

The day after Cameron's departure from our ranks to destinations unknown was the day we went to get our basic issue clothing. Once again we were all made to go through an assembly line process. Every time we would take a step, somebody would size us up and stuff a new article of clothing into our newly-acquired duffel bags. By the time we reached the end of the warehouse, we each had two duffel bags stuffed to the brim with uniforms, boots, belts, and equipment.

That was where I met Private Jameson for the first time. It was one of those situations where you meet someone and instantly there is animosity between the two of you. Jameson was one of those annoyingly perfect people, the kind that cartoonists model super heroes after. What really got to me was his eyes. There was something about the way he looked at me when we first met. It gave me the feeling I had seen those very eyes staring back at me from somewhere and, frankly, it made my skin crawl. I tried my best to like him, but for some reason I just couldn't make myself do it. He seemed too stuck up, like he knew something that I didn't, and he was very standoffish. And to make matters worse, he was quite the show off. It was almost as if we were destined to be at odds with each other. Looking back, I now know the reason he acted the way he did, but I didn't figure it out until several years later.

The second program of basic is the actual training. On the first day of our fourth week in reception, we were told to get all of our gear packed. At twenty-two hundred hours we were loaded onto a bus and shipped to our training billets. The bus ride lasted almost an hour and a half from start to finish. We were all certain that they had taken us to a completely different installation altogether. Later on, we discovered that the reception area and the training areas were only a mile and a half apart and that our driver was told to confuse us on our way in.

The training program was broken down into three phases: red, white, and blue. During the red phase, everyone was to blame for everything, no matter how trivial. We received the maximum punishment every time. This was the phase in which the drill sergeant's only goal was to break us down and build us back up as soldiers. Every morning at o-dark-thirty, Drill Sergeant Hobbs would walk into the bay and start to count to three. When he reached three, we were supposed to be standing shoulder to shoulder around the bay, so we could be counted. This was called "toeing the line" because we placed our toes on a long line that circled the entire room. Our first morning there he counted very loud and very fast. Needless to say we didn't make it in time. Our punishment for not meeting the standard was to get "smoked," meaning that we had to do whatever exercise the drill sergeant wanted us to do until he was satisfied that we were tired and had learned our lesson. We were smoked for about thirty minutes for that first infraction. After we had completed our sentence, we were sent outside to do our daily scheduled morning PT, which was a grueling two hours of running in formation all over the post.

Upon completion of our little jog, we were directed back up to our barracks to get ready for the day. On our way up the stairs the drill sergeant called out, "You have only five minutes to shower, shave, shine, and shampoo! After that you had better be in formation and ready for chow!"

Not wanting to be the cause of another smoke session, I had immediately gone into panic mode and started to rush up the stairs. This only helped to confirm the fact that we were indeed cattle at that time, for I was not the only one following that line of thought. The resulting stampede of sweating, stinking soldier wannabees only served to slow down our overall progress, and fifteen minutes later, we were out in the grass, getting smoked. Again. The rest of the day was pretty much the same thing. We were given a simple task to do with an unreasonably short time period to do it in, and then we were punished for the failure. Drill Sergeant Hobbs' catch phrase quickly became, "Get in the grass!" This was immediately followed by a variety of commands for numerous exercises. The only good thing about that first full day of training was that we slept like the dead that night.

The next morning we were determined not to get smoked for being slow getting out of bed. One of the guys set his watch alarm for four twenty-five, got out of his bunk, and proceeded to get everyone out of bed. We were so sure that this was what we had to do to meet the standard that we were completely dumbstruck when we saw our drill sergeant's reaction. When he walked in and saw that we were out of bed waiting for him, he completely lost his mind. For the next hour and forty-five minutes we had the pleasure of learning all sorts of new exercise techniques, the whole time wondering what we had done wrong.

Two weeks into training we had finally become acclimated to our schedule. Wake up. Get smoked. Head outside for PT. Run upstairs to get cleaned up. Get smoked for being too slow and finally head out again for our daily training.

That was when Drill Sergeant Hobbs decided to throw us a curve ball. He walked into the bay and started counting down from five, slowly. By the time he had reached two we were all "toeing the line" and waiting to count off. After we had verified that we were all present and accounted for, we found out why our morning routine had changed. It was to be the first day of basic rifle marksmanship, and he wanted to have us ready early.

When we had completed our daily fitness routine and choked down yet another culinary mystery, we were formed up in platoon formation and given serialized arms cards. One by one we filed through the armory and exchanged our arms card for our personal M16. We were so excited about being able to shoot something that we completely lost our military composure and started talking amongst ourselves. That was a huge mistake. We didn't realize how big a mistake it was until we heard those four dreadful words–"GET IN THE GRASS!!" We quickly learned that getting smoked with an M16 in your hands is much worse than without.

For four days we trained with our rifles. We were taught how to disassemble, reassemble, clean, and carry the M16 in a professional manner. On the fifth day, we were marched two miles out to the ranges and issued our first forty rounds of ammunition. We were given extensive lessons on range safety then marched single file out to the firing points.

One of the range rules was to keep the muzzle of the weapon elevated and pointed down range. This was the first rule that was broken, and thankfully the last.

One of the privates, three firing points down from me, had a malfunction with his rifle and had decided to go about fixing the problem on his own. It was just a simple jam, a very common problem with basic training weapons because they received so much abuse during each cycle. The private started doing what he had been trained to do to clear the jam. He started chanting the mantra to himself, and time seemed to slow down. "Slap, Pull, Observe, Release, Tap, and Squeeze." When he said "slap," he deftly slapped the bottom of the magazine. When he said "pull" and "observe," he swung the muzzle of his weapon to his left and yanked back on the charging handle to remove the bad round from the chamber and watched it fall to the ground. When he said "release," he released the charging handle and the next round in the magazine was locked and loaded into the chamber. As he said "tap" and slammed his palm against the forward assist knob, one of the closest range NCOs saw what he was doing and started to run for the potentially homicidal individual. Just as the NCO reached him, the private said "squeeze," completely forgot which way his weapon was pointed, and squeezed the trigger. Having been expertly cleared of the jam and reloaded, the weapon discharged, not downrange in the proper direction, but back and to the left, directly at one of the drill sergeants. Luckily for the drill sergeant, the round only grazed the back of his thighs, putting four neat little holes in the back of his uniform pants just above the knees. When all was said and done, the total casualty count was four: one pair of uniform pants, two pairs of underwear, and the military career of one careless private.

The beginning of white phase brought with it some welcome changes. First of all, group punishment was becoming less and less frequent and more attention was placed on the individual. Second, the drill sergeants were starting to loosen up a bit. We had even heard Drill Sergeant Hobbs crack a joke. It wasn't the cleanest joke, and therefore I can't repeat it, but it still proved that he was human. The most anticipated change was the beginning of our hand-to-hand combat training.

The hand-to-hand combat taught by the army isn't the flashiest fighting style in the world. The best description is "an extremely violent form of wrestling." The closest martial art form to this style would probably be jujitsu. Whatever they wanted to call it, I loved it. They were giving us the perfect opportunity to settle our disputes amongst ourselves. Up until that point Jameson and I hadn't had a chance to settle our differences, and I planned to make full use of it.

Challenge day was the only day that the trainees could call out anyone we wanted to and settle our differences, one-on-one, with hand-to-hand combat. The day started well enough. One of the other drill sergeants challenged ours and did surprisingly well for about thirty seconds. We soon learned why our drill sergeant was the hand-to-hand instructor for our company.

About an hour after the challenges started, it was my turn to issue a challenge. I made my way to the center of the circle and pointed to Jameson. He calmly rose to his feet and joined me in the circle. The drill sergeant had known that there was some animosity between us and had been expecting that to happen. He grabbed both of us by the shoulders and whispered to us, "I know you two have some bad blood between you, just don't spill too much of it."

The sparring match started like all others. We were both told to start on our knees and not to throw punches at each others' faces. Everything else was fair game. As soon as Drill Sergeant Hobbs said *Go*, we locked up on each other. We struggled for what seemed like hours trying to push each other off balance. I felt him pushing harder and harder against my arms trying to push me over. When I felt that the moment was right, I pulled with all of my strength, placed a foot on his stomach, and kicked hard. Jameson literally flew through the air and landed on his back, dazed. I executed a perfect backwards somersault and landed on his chest, determined not to lose the fight. As I fought to grab onto his collar to try and choke him out, I could hear Drill Sergeant Hobbs actually cheering for me. I had known for sure that I was going to win that fight when I started, and nothing was going to stop m–

"All right, Martin, that's enough. You know as well as I do that the fight didn't last very long and was nowhere near that exciting. You might as well just tell them how it ended and get it over with."

"As you wish, Sir"

As I fought for control of Jameson's collar, I failed to keep control of his legs. He wrapped them around my torso, flipped me over, and quickly choked me into unconsciousness. It was as if he knew exactly when and how to press his advantage. Even though I had the upper hand in the beginning of the fight, it seemed he knew what moves I was going to make and, more importantly, what mistakes I was going to make. The official fight time, from start to finish, was somewhere in the neighborhood of twenty to twenty-five seconds. That night I made a silent pledge to even the score between us. The perfect opportunity– the pugil competition–was only three weeks away.

The final phase of basic training was the most fun of the three. All of the group punishments were gone, and we were focusing on the more technical details of being a soldier. These details included land navigation, first aid, confidence building, obstacle courses, and bayonet training. But the highlight of blue phase was the pugil training and competition.

The pugil competition was probably the biggest fighting competition on Fort Jackson. We were paired up amongst ourselves with trainees of about the same build. As with hand-to-hand combat training, we were told to try and settle our differences on the field and not to carry them back to the barracks. Only this time we were using large padded sticks called pugils and trying to score points, not render our opponents unconscious. The rules were simple; the first person to score three points would win the match and advance to the next round. Points were awarded when one person struck their opponent in either the head or the torso. We were told that the overall winner of the day would get to skip the morning run the next day. Needless to say, we were quite motivated.

The first match of the day was between two of our smallest compatriots, and like two lightweight boxers the fighting was fast and intense. One combatant would attack, and the other would block and counterattack. The battle lasted about three and a half minutes with a final score of two to three. The next fight was between our two biggest colleagues. As the titans faced off against each other, we had all settled in for a long drawn out fight. Surprisingly, the fight was over in only a few seconds. The first attack was so

powerful that it was the only one needed. In fact, the force
of the blow was so great that it broke the pugil and rendered
the recipient unconscious. Neither individual was allowed to
compete in any more pugil events.

When Jameson's event came around, I realized the only
way I would be able to settle the score between us is if he
won, so naturally I started rooting for him to win. I figured
that if anyone was going to get the best of Jameson, it was
going to be me. Jameson was paired off against Private Smith
for his first match. As the two started to circle each other, it
dawned on me that I should try to study his tactics and learn
his weaknesses. Jameson struck first, landing a blow squarely
on top of Smith's helmet. The second attack was issued from
Smith in the form of a jab to the stomach. With the score tied
one to one, the gladiators began circling the ring once more.
They were fairly evenly matched, and I had begun to worry
that Smith might be able to beat Jameson and therefore ruin
my chance at retribution. The next exchange was a lightning
barrage of attacks and counterattacks that were so fast that
even the drill sergeant had a hard time keeping up. When the
combatants finally separated, they each had one additional
point.

During the match I learned that Jameson favored
the overhead attacks, using his height and strength to his
advantage. On more than one occasion he had locked up with
Smith after such an attack. Smith, also favoring brute force,
had just pushed up and back, trying to throw Jameson off
balance, a move which usually ended in stalemate. I now had
an idea how to best Jameson. Only two things could have
prevented me from putting that theory to the test. If he lost to
Smith, he would be disqualified. Also, I had to fight someone
else to advance and be able to face him in the second round.

The third and final point of the duel between Jameson
and Smith came as quite a surprise to all of us. During

a torrent of attacks and counterattacks, Jameson lost his balance, stumbled backwards, tripped, and landed flat on his back. Smith, sensing victory, launched himself into the air with his pugil held high over his head intending to club Jameson into the ground and subsequently out of the competition. Time seemed to slow down. I felt my hopes of retribution being smashed with every inch of ground Smith flew over in his theatrical final assault on Jameson. Everyone watching the match was on their feet screaming at the top of their lungs. Even the drill sergeants had all started cheering for their favorite competitor. I had just given up my last shred of hope when Smith's victory cry ended very abruptly. A hush had fallen over the crowd, and nobody could believe their eyes. Even the drill sergeants were rendered speechless by the spectacle. At the last possible moment, Jameson had placed one end of his pugil into the dirt between his legs and had positioned the other end directly beneath Smith's oncoming torso. Smith's victory cry had ended as he landed on the end of Jameson's pugil and knocked the wind out of himself. Smith seemed to balance on top of the pugil stick for what seemed like an eternity, until Jameson finally pushed him over. The roar of the crowd was so loud it was reportedly heard all the way to base headquarters.

My first bout was against Private Devore. Devore was a nondescript and quiet individual about five feet eight inches tall with a medium build. I had so much confidence that I was going to beat Devore hands down, that I was caught completely off guard when he scored the first point with a simple jab. The fact that I let my ego get the better of me made me boiling mad, not at Devore, but at myself. I was not going to let that little pip-squeak ruin my chances of vengeance just because I failed to see him for what he was. I forced myself to see Devore not as a person but as

an obstacle which I had to surmount in order to achieve my
goal. I worked myself into a frothing, seething rage and
charged. With every bit of skill I could muster I blew through
his defenses and scored a coup on his face shield.

In response to my strike, he made a raging charge of his
own. He showed considerable skill with the pugil, and very
quickly had me retreating around the ring. Time after time
he landed blows against my pugil, pushing me back toward
the onlookers behind me. Just as I had begun to think I was
going to lose after all, an opportunity presented itself. Devore
stepped into small depression and briefly lost his balance.
That was all it took to turn the tide in my favor. As he started
to stumble, I sidestepped him to the left, hooked my pugil
on his and with all of my might twisted, shoved, and pried
the pugil out of his hands. The discarded weapon was flung
into the crowd, well out of the reach of poor Devore. If I had
been fighting only him, and not in a tournament, I would
have allowed him to retrieve his pugil, however, I could not
allow him to have any chance to stop me on my quest to face
Jameson. I quickly scored a hit to his stomach, swept his feet
out from under him and unceremoniously jabbed him in the
face shield for my final point.

As I stood over top of my vanquished foe, relief flowed
over me. I had overcome the last obstacle in my quest for
vindication against Jameson, or so I thought. Little did I
know, fate had used that discarded pugil stick to thwart my
plans once again. When the staff had been torn from Devore's
grip and flung through the air it had struck Private Bryant;
the biggest, meanest, and scariest trainee in our platoon. To
say the least, he was a bit upset. After my match with Devore,
I watched as Bryant spoke to the drill sergeant in charge of
the events, and wondered why he was scowling at me during
the brief exchange. The drill sergeant nodded in agreement,
eliciting a smile on Bryant's face. The smile replaced the

scowl, but somehow made him appear much more menacing than before. Out of curiosity, I wandered over in his general direction and tried to discern what had happened to get me on his hit list. I watched as he put on his protective gear for his first match, and decided to stick around to watch the beating that was about to ensue. The unfortunate individual who had the luck to draw Bryant as his first opponent never even had a chance to swing his pugil. Bryant made such quick work of his first round pick that he volunteered to start his second round fight right away. The drill sergeant hadn't seen any problem with this and called out the next contender.

Bryant's second match was pretty much the same as his first. The challenger approached the center of the ring with the march of a man condemned to the gallows, tapped his pugil against Bryant's, and attempted to endure the beating that soon commenced. As Bryant delivered blow after blow to his opponent's defenses, it became painfully obvious who was going to win the match. To give his opposition credit, he never did give up. He fought as if his life depended on it, as it may very well have, deflecting as many blows as possible.

When the dust settled and Bryant was firmly under control, everyone gathered to see what had become of the challenger. Lying in the middle of the pugil pit was a whimpering, quivering mass of a trainee. Unfortunately, I was that trainee. As I laid there trying to gather the strength to stand, I felt all hope of ever facing my one true nemesis slip away. Two of my fellow companions came to my side, helped me to my feet, and escorted me over to the bleachers where all the other eliminated individuals had congregated. For the remainder of the day I was in a perpetual fog, not knowing what had transpired to make the fates turn against me in such a way and wondering if my entire career would turn out the same way, always building up to something great

only to have my feet yanked out from under me at the last
possible second.

        The last week of basic training brought a unique
experience. Some people called it a camping trip; some
called it cruel and unusual punishment. The Army calls
it Victory Forge. Victory Forge is a five-day, four-night,
twenty-six-kilometer excursion into the back woods of Fort
Jackson carrying eighty pounds of gear on your back and an
M-16 in your hands. We were told that it would require the
use of all our new skills to succeed on this expedition and
make it back for graduation. We were going to be tested on
stamina, accuracy with a rifle, the ability to repel attacks,
and the ability to react to an ever changing war simulation
environment. And tested we were.
        Our first test of the week was one of accuracy. We
started out at three in the morning and marched about five
kilometers at a fairly quick pace. Our first destination was the
qualification range for our last chance to put live ammunition
through our rifles and kill as many little plastic men as
possible. We were issued forty rounds and told to make every
one count. Fortunately for me, accuracy wasn't too much
of a problem. I was able to eliminate thirty-six out of forty
polymer foes. With the average score of the platoon around
twenty-eight, I felt quite good about my score. I cleared my
weapon and made my way to the holding area to await the
next leg of our journey. As I stood waiting for the rest of
the platoon to finish their qualification, I heard a cheer erupt
from the firing line. One of my colleagues had made a perfect
score, and had earned the title eagle-eye. Eager to see who
had made the best score in the company, we all made our way
up to the range exit. Much to my chagrin, the best shot in the
company was none other than Private Jameson.
        Our second test was one of stamina. We were marched

the remaining twenty-one kilometers through sand, gravel, and ditches, uphill and down, and finally into a densely wooded area. To our credit, none of the soldiers in our company fell out of the march on the way to the campsite.

Upon our arrival at Victory Forge, we were issued two hundred and ten rounds of blank ammunition and were told to set up our tents and our defenses. We were also told to be on the lookout for an imminent attack from an unknown foe.

With our first priority being defense, my battle buddy, Private Gamblin, and I started to dig our foxhole. Our drill sergeant enlightened us on the proper way to measure a foxhole. He informed us that it had to be two M16s long, one M16 wide and chest deep, and if we managed to get that far in our construction, then we could worry about camouflaging it. Within a few hours, the two of us had not only dug our foxhole deep enough, we had also carved stairs out of the dirt behind it in order to effect a quicker escape in case of a grenade attack. It was at that point that we decided to go and eat some of the MREs, or Meals Ready to Eat, that we had brought along with us.

After we had consumed our dinner rations, Gamblin decided that he would take care of the trash. In the process of doing so, he inadvertently discovered how to make a tear gas bomb out of the MRE pouch. When he had finished his meal, he had dumped everything into the heavy duty outer wrapper in order to gather up all of his waste. Included in his refuse was an open Tabasco bottle and a used MRE heater. He had then proceeded to stuff his bag of trash tightly into my bag of trash, walk over to the large garbage bag and stuff the mass of litter deep into the bag. The MRE heater, having been exposed to water and then Tabasco sauce, continued to produce heat and hydrogen gas, quickly pressurizing the two MRE bags it was stuffed into until the bags could no longer stand the pressure. The resulting explosion blew trash and debris all around the campsite along with a large cloud of vaporized hot sauce, causing quite a few people to don their gas masks and run to their foxholes, believing that we were under attack. Knowing exactly what had transpired and not wanting to get into trouble for it, we had thrown on our own masks and made a hasty retreat to our foxhole as well. The drill sergeants never did figure out who had blown up the trash bag.

That night we decided to finish building our foxhole during our guard watch. As Gamblin stood the first watch, I snuck over to the drill sergeant's supply pile and gathered up as many five-foot-long steel bars as I could carry. We used the bars to build a slanting cage over the top of our foxhole and then piled sandbags on top of that. When we finished the structure, we agreed that we needed to camouflage the entire thing in order to minimize our chances of getting tear gassed while on watch. As luck would have it, when everyone had cleared the area for their foxholes, they had piled all of the sticks and pine needles directly behind our area. We used the entire pile to disguise our foxhole, and when we were finished, nobody even knew there was a foxhole there. We concealed our position so well that when the drill sergeant came out to simulate an attack, he tripped over the side sandbag wall and fell on top of our roof. Had we been awake at the time we would have probably seen him coming and stopped him, but we were both so worn out from all the marching and digging that we had fallen asleep in the fox hole. When the drill sergeant landed on the roof, we both came out screaming. Lucky for us he thought it was a war cry instead of a terrified screech and quickly surrendered. We were both congratulated on having the best fighting position in the company.

The following night the first real attack came. At about zero two hundred, a mortar simulator whistled loudly through the camp and everyone sprang to their posts. As we watched the night intently we began to see some movement in the field directly in front of us. Two men in dark clothing were standing about three feet apart with something stretched taut between them. A third individual stepped up to what we later learned was a giant slingshot, loaded a second mortar simulator, and let it fly toward our camp. Shouts of "Incoming" echoed throughout the camp. The soldiers in the foxhole to our right opened fire on the mortar position and gave away their position to the mortar men. The third round landed directly in their foxhole, and unlike the first two which were mortar simulators, this one was a tear gas grenade. As soon as we heard the other privates coughing I knew they were in trouble. I told Gamblin to put on his mask and open fire on the mortar men so I could go and help our fallen friends. I put on my mask and ran over to the other foxhole as fast as I could. The two soldiers inside were so overcome by the gas that they hadn't even been able to put on their masks and were blindly trying to get out of their hole. I reached down into the cloud of tear gas, grabbed onto the first soldier by the belt and hauled him out. I reached back down into the hole, got ahold of his battle buddy, and hauled him out as well. To my surprise, the second soldier I pulled out of the hole was none other than Private Jameson. To tell the truth, the thought of just dropping him back into the hole did cross my mind, but I decided that it wasn't fair to beat up someone who was blinded by tear gas and had tears and snot running down his face. When I had made sure that neither of them were seriously injured, I escorted them back to the tree line so they could recover without getting any more exposure.

When I arrived back at our foxhole, I found Gamblin seething mad. He was screaming all sorts of obscenities as well as multiple references to our attackers' family lineages, and he finally decided to go and do something about the whole mess. I watched in awe as Gamblin executed his simple yet highly effective plan. He quickly exited the foxhole, removed his gas mask, and let out an ear splitting whistle. Had that been a real life attack and not a training exercise, he would have been shot by an enemy rifleman as soon as he stepped into view. However, since it was training, the only ammunition that was effective against us was the tear gas grenades. The mortar men loaded up another grenade and let it fly directly at my battle buddy. As soon as the grenade was in the air, Gamblin picked up a large stick and wielded it like a Louisville Slugger, and with a loud grunt swung as hard as he could. The improvised baseball bat connected with the irritating projectile and sent it flying back toward the attackers at the precise moment it started to release its contents, creating a smoking tracer round that landed squarely at their feet. The cloud of gas quickly enveloped their improvised fighting position. and they were forced to retreat into the trees behind them.

As soon as the attackers vacated their position, Gamblin executed stage two of his plan. He put his mask back on and ran across the field and into the cloud. When he returned to our fighting position, he was carrying a large burlap sack and a three man slingshot. I never did figure out what stage three of his plan was going to be. It was at that precise moment that our drill sergeant decided to come congratulate the hero of the night and subsequently caught him with the bag of mortar simulators and tear gas grenades. Thinking quickly on his feet, he handed over the bag and told the drill sergeant that he had successfully overrun the enemy position and secured all of their weapons as spoils of war. The drill sergeant took the grenades, patted him on the back and mumbled something about everyone wanting to be a hero before heading back toward the center of the camp.

For the next forty-eight hours we were attacked relentlessly. It seemed as though the attackers were trying to punish us for our successful repulsion of their first attack. They had even changed their tactics. Instead of using their slingshot to lob in the grenades, they were taping them to small radio controlled cars and driving them through the camp. After the third attack with the cars, we began to smash their cars with our shovels. When we had broken all of their toys, they launched the worst attack of all. At least six men who were dressed in black fatigues, gas masks, and backpacks walked through our camp with tear gas grenades taped onto the ends of sticks. The gas was so thick by the end of the attack that some of the trainees had a hard time seeing where they were going and fell into foxholes. Luckily, nobody was seriously hurt.

The last day of our field training exercise was fairly uneventful, which was a good thing because we were worn out. We spent the majority of the day filling in our foxholes and packing up our equipment. We were told to try to relax until sundown for our hike back to the barracks. When it came time for the long trek back, we all gathered our gear and assembled into two single file lines, one on either side of the road. On the command given by our drill sergeant, we began the slow, weary, depressing, yet determined walk of men who have nothing left in life except the impulse to simply sol–

"Sir, I believe that if you use that last line you will be committing plagiarism."
"Nonsense, Martin, I just made that up."

"No, Sir, you did not. The quote that you just used comes from an old movie that was released in the year two thousand and one under the title of A Knight's Tale. *There was a scene with a naked man walking down a dirt road and he was asked what he was doing–"*

"What's your point?"

"Although the writers probably would not make too much of a fuss over a single line, there is always the potential for legal issues when you copy someone's work."

"All right, all right. If it will make you feel better, I will put some kind of reference page at the end of the book with all the quotes that you believe I have used along with their sources. Why should it matter to you if I get into any legal trouble anyway?"

"It matters, Sir, because you once told me to stick around to try and keep you out of trouble. And I intend to do that, no matter how trivial you think it might be."

"I did say that, didn't I. Thank you, Martin. I am not sure where I would be without your wisdom and guidance."

"I could show you if you would like."

"No, no, no, that won't be necessary. The last time you did that I couldn't sleep for a week!"

As we trudged down the road I began to notice a strange phenomenon. Slowly, like an orchestra tuning up before a show, everyone had started marching in step with each other until the only sound that could be heard was the steady thumping of two hundred and forty pairs of boots impacting the dirt at the same time. I too had found it impossible to march out of step. Every time I tried, my feet just fell back into rhythm. Another thing I noticed was the blank stares and slack expressions on everyone's faces. They were all staring at the back of the helmet of the person in front of them and most of them weren't even blinking. Wondering what could have possibly enraptured most, if not all, of my comrades, I decided to do a little experiment. I took a deep breath, let all of my facial muscles go slack, and gazed deeply at the back of the helmet in front of me. I noticed two things almost immediately. The first thing was the straps around the helmets had two little squares on them that faintly glowed in the dark. I later learned that they were called cat eyes. The second thing I noticed was that they seemed to be swelling rapidly. I watched with absolute amazement as the squares grew larger and larger. When they filled my vision completely it became painfully clear what had happened. It hit me like a freight train, or more appropriately, like a helmet to the face. We had all fallen asleep during the journey. When we arrived at our destination and the leaders of the two lines came to a stop, everyone behind them, one after the other, walked into the back of the person in front of them causing everyone to fall over like dominoes. When the drill sergeants turned around and saw us piled up like an overturned bucket of green plastic soldiers, they all started laughing hysterically. That is, all except Drill Sergeant Jackson. He removed a twenty dollar bill from his wallet, gave it to Drill Sergeant Hobbs, and just walked away.

When we had extricated ourselves from the pile and the drill sergeants had composed themselves, the first sergeant came out of his office to congratulate us on our successful completion of Victory Forge. He described in vivid detail the order of events for the graduation ceremony that was scheduled for the next day, and we quickly learned how to use our new-found talent of sleep marching while standing still. He lectured us for about an hour before he dismissed us to go shower and retire to bed.

Graduation day started off rather nicely. Since we had just finished marching home from Victory Forge at two a.m.

that morning, we were allowed to skip the morning exercise and sleep in til eight o'clock. After chow we spent the next four hours practicing how to stand still during speeches and then march around the parade field. The whole time during practice, the one thing they kept drilling into our heads was not to lock our knees during the ceremony. After lunch we were marched to the barracks to put on our dress uniforms and get ready for graduation. When we had all changed into our dress greens, we were subjected to a surprise inspection by the command sergeant major, who just walked around our bay and straightened a few ties before moving on to the next platoon. When all of the training staff was convinced that we had successfully dressed ourselves, we were loaded onto the buses and taken to the parade field on the far side of post. That's where the nice part of the day ended.

Nestled between hills, tall trees, and large buildings, the small shaded clearing that we had practiced on had seemed rather nice that day. Added to the fact that we were wearing loose-fitting duty uniforms, one could call it quite pleasant. But when we arrived at the parade field wearing heavy wool dress uniforms on the hottest day of the year, we realized that graduation was going to be just one more test we had to endure.

"Sir, it was late October when you graduated, well past the hottest time of the year."
"Martin, this is my story. Let me tell it the way I want to."
"As you wish, Sir."

When we had formed up into a block formation our drill sergeant marched us out to our spot on the parade field. With everyone in position and the sun glaring down from overhead, the speeches began. The first speaker was the post commander and his fifteen minute discourse was the shortest one of the day. By the time the third speaker finished, we were already an hour into the ceremony. When the fourth "honored guest" approached the podium to give his account of our training progress, an odd noise attracted my attention. It sounded very much like a large bag of sand being dropped on the ground. Since we were standing at attention, I wasn't allowed to move my head to find the source of the sound but I was fairly certain it came from behind me and to the right. I listened intently for a few seconds more and the sound repeated itself, only this time it was behind and to my left. I wasn't exactly sure what I was hearing until our first squad leader, who just happened to be Private Bryant, started to sway back and forth as if to some strange song. With a groan that sounded like the protests of a felled tree, Bryant tipped backwards and landed squarely on top of the smallest person in our company, Private Butler. Both trainees were quickly retrieved by the medics who had been circling behind our formation like sharks since we started. Bryant and a large number of others were treated for heat related injuries, while Butler was treated for a sprained wrist and a twisted knee from being crushed. The rest of us went on to complete the graduation ritual with the pass and review, where we marched around the field to be inspected by the top brass and then back to our starting point. When everyone had completed the circuit, we heard the one order that we had been waiting for since the start of training, "DISMISSED!"

Unlike many college graduation ceremonies, we didn't throw our military head gear into the air. We did, however, scatter like roaches when someone turns on the lights. In the midst of all the confusion I tried to find the one person that I wouldn't exactly miss, but still wanted one last shot at, Private Jameson. Strangely enough, as soon as we were dismissed he had just disappeared. Some of the guys said they had seen him talking with some high-brass official, but nobody knew of his current whereabouts. It wasn't until several years later that I would find out what had become of Private Jameson.

Chapter 2
Soldier in Training

After the graduation ceremonies, all of the trainees were separated into groups based on their military professions, and just by looking around I could easily tell where each group was destined to go. The infantry trainees were standing in formation, discussing the best ways to care for an M16 rifle, the linguists were huddled in a group speaking in tongues, the light wheel mechanics were trying to suck up to the drill sergeant by rotating his tires, and the spec ops guys were hiding in the tree line. As for myself, I was with the potential aircraft crew chiefs sitting on a bench, waiting for the bus ride to take us to our next training station.

Upon arrival at Fort Eustis, we were all anxious to get off the bus, and in our haste to depart, we accidentally trampled the corporal who was assigned to take us to our billets. Our preconceived notion that nothing could be worse than upsetting a drill sergeant was shattered, along with most of our personal records for the most push-ups done in a single session.

"You know, Martin, we probably wouldn't have had to do as many push-ups as we wound up doing had we been able to stop laughing at that poor corporal."

"Sir, what could you have possibly found humorous about running over a junior NCO?"

"We just found it extremely difficult to take him seriously when he was covered in boot prints and turning so many different shades of red." David laughed so hard that he fell into a coughing fit.

"I will never understand your sense of humor, Sir."

When we had satisfied the corporal's need to avenge himself, we were escorted to our new training barracks. As we were marched up to the Bravo Company parking lot, we were met by a very irate drill sergeant, Drill Sergeant Shining, who was to become our platoon sergeant during the first few weeks of our training. Physically, he wasn't a very big person. Most of the trainees believed that if he hadn't been wearing thick socks on the day he joined, he wouldn't have made the minimum height requirement for the army. Unfortunately, as with most people in a position of authority possessing his diminutive stature, he had a severe case of Napoleon Syndrome.

The next few weeks were an absolute nightmare for us. Every night we were subjected to various inspections with impossible standards. Those who failed to meet those standards, and there were quite a few of us, spent the rest of the night outside doing whatever exercise Drill Sergeant Shining deemed appropriate for our punishment. The only escape from his wrath was to volunteer for CQ, or Charge of Quarters duty.

On one of those rare occasions that I was allowed to work at the CQ desk, I had the opportunity to speak with the drill sergeant from one of the other platoons, Drill Sergeant Bratton. I expressed my desire to move out of the newbie platoon and asked if there was any way that I could possibly be assigned to his platoon. His response was one that filled me with hope and once again set me on a course for disaster.

"Private, if you want to get out of Drill Sergeant Shining's platoon, you are going to have to do something that will make you stand out from the rest of the soldiers who want to be transferred."

As he had spoken those words a chill of excitement had passed up my spine, and with one simple question I committed myself to a course that would change not only my current circumstances, but also the military careers of several other individuals.

"What would you suggest that I do, Drill Sergeant?"

"Well, Private, every cycle Charlie Company has been sending a small task force over into our company area to steal our company guide-on, and every cycle we have to send one back to retrieve it. Those individuals who volunteer are looked upon quite favorably, unless they are caught."

"What do they do with our guide-on when they take it, Drill Sergeant? And if I successfully retrieve it, will you get me transferred into your platoon? "

"They usually display it in the open where everyone can keep an eye on it, and they always post guards. If you can get it, I will get your transfer. Of course they haven't stolen it yet, so you will just have to wait until they do."

I didn't have to wait long. Three days after my talk with Drill Sergeant Bratton, Charlie Company made their move. Sometime during the early morning hours a small task force consisting of four people entered our company area and stole our company guide-on. To make matters worse, nobody noticed until we were all in formation getting ready to head out to school.

Our company guide-on was nothing more than a small royal blue cotton flag with a set of golden aviation wings and propeller embroidered on it. It was hung from a seven foot hickory pole that mounted into a flagpole holder. What made the flag special was the level of security that we were forced to maintain around it. To begin with, we had a six foot square area that was painted bright yellow, called a kill-zone, which the flag never left unless it was carried in front of the company formation during a battalion run or en route to school. This area was inspected every five to ten minutes by a roving guard, usually a new private fresh from basic awaiting a class slot, and randomly by the drill sergeant on duty. When the guards would inspect the area, their main objective was to ensure that nobody had walked through the kill zone or tampered with the guide-on.

Since the shiny yellow paint showed boot prints extremely well, and the area was lit up by four very bright spot lights, none of the guards ever really went too close to the kill zone to do their inspection. It was because of that complacency that the Charlie Company task force was able to pull off their coup. While one private distracted the guards, three young men dressed in black clothing crept up to our guide-on and switched it out for something that looked very similar from a distance but was obviously not the genuine article upon closer inspection. To avoid leaving their boot prints on the "kill-zone," they laid down a trail of paper towels and just walked across to the flag.

As our guide-on bearer approached the kill-zone, he noticed something wasn't quite right about the flag. In the place of our guide-on, stapled to a hickory flagpole, was a pair of blue cotton boxer shorts with a picture of a large yellow canary on them. The senior drill sergeant was so furious with the guards who were on night shift that he went into the barracks and pulled each and every one of them out of bed and started smoking them in the parking lot as we were leaving for school, and those poor privates were still being drilled when we came back for lunch.

That evening as I was lying in my bunk, I started formulating a plan to get the guide-on back. As Drill Sergeant Bratton had said, they were displaying our flag in plain sight, directly in front of their drill sergeant's office window. In order for my plan to work I would need a lot of luck, three willing participants and a few miscellaneous items. I had just started to draw out my plans when Drill Sergeant Bratton knocked on my door. I jumped to my feet and stood at parade rest and awaited further instructions.

"As you were, Private. Are you still willing to try and retrieve our property?"

"Yes I am, Drill Sergeant. I was just drawing up the plans now. I will probably have to recruit about three people to help pull it off though."

"If you can be ready to move in about an hour I will have three participants for you. Just don't get caught, and if you do, I don't know anything about your plans."

"I understand, Drill Sergeant."

One hour later I was pleasantly surprised to discover that all three volunteers were on the night shift guard duty when the guide-on was stolen. Drill Sergeant Bratton had cut them a deal to get them off the "S" list in exchange for their services. He even provided a couple of items I required for our raid against the enemy encampment. These items included a small but extremely loud alarm clock, a laser pointer, a toilet paper tube, some five-fifty cord, and the offending undergarment that had been set in place of our flag. I took about fifteen minutes to go over the plan with my squad, and then we made our way out of the barracks.

The plan was extremely simple and consisted of three steps for our primary objectives and two secondary objectives. Our first step was to create a disturbance that would distract not only the guards but also the drill sergeant in the office. Step two was to infiltrate the Charlie Company courtyard and secure our guide-on. Our final step was to successfully return to our own company area. The secondary objectives were thought up on the spot and they were to steal their guide-on and to repay them for their joke on us.

When we arrived at the Charlie Company parking lot, I

sent one of the privates off to set up the laser pointer and the toilet paper tube on the farthest end of the courtyard from the drill sergeant's office window. He set the tube down in a high branch of a tree and looked through it like a sight, aiming it at the office window. He then placed the laser pointer inside the tube, turned it on, making sure it was shining through the window, and then made his way back to our position, all without being seen. While he was setting up the laser, I went about recruiting the fifth and final member of our squad.

Two weeks prior to the theft of our flag, the Charlie Company First Sergeant had "adopted" a stray cat that he found outside their chow hall. He went as far as building a small house for it to live in and even bought it a food and water dish, which was kept stocked at all times. The cat was given a collar and the name Sergeant Major Cat.

After I had captured the cat, I set about the task of dressing it in the boxer shorts using the five-fifty cord as suspenders to keep them on. I also set the alarm for twenty minutes and used another piece of cord to attach it to the feline.

"Sir, I believe tying objects to a cat, or any animal for that matter, is considered animal cruelty. And being proud of that act could be construed as a major character flaw."

"Martin, desperate times called for desperate measures. If tying a few harmless items to that flea-ridden fur ball was going to get me out of the hellfire platoon, then I was going to do what I had to do. We were being smothered. We were being abused. We were being repressed. WE NEEDED BREATHING ROOM!!" David collapsed onto his couch in a coughing fit, having worked himself up during his tirade.

"Hitler said the very same thing in 1938."

"What was that, Martin?"

"Nothing, Sir."
"Humph."

When the laser was set and the cat fully dressed, we made our way to the back door of the barracks and put the cat inside. When the drill sergeant noticed the red dot from the laser on his wall, he left his office to investigate the source. Had he waited thirty more seconds he would have seen the cat coming down the hall, and our plans would have been ruined, but for the first time I could remember, my luck held. The Drill Sergeant made his way out the front door and enlisted the help of the guards to track down the source of the laser. Since the laser was set so high off the ground and was shrouded by the cardboard tube, it proved surprisingly difficult for them to find. Just as they were closing in on its location, the second part of our distraction went prominently into effect.

Private Susan Maryweather had just completed her rotation at the CQ desk and was enjoying the first hot shower she had had in a long time. She was in her late twenties with the barest hint of red in her blonde hair. After her boss had cashed out his business and left her high and dry, she had gone against the only advice he had given her before he left and had joined the army.

Sergeant Major Cat, complete with alarm clock and boxers, wandered into the female latrine just as Private Maryweather started washing her hair. Her off-key singing piqued his curiosity and he walked right into the shower stall with her. She didn't even notice the cat until the alarm on his back went off with a high-pitched shriek, sending the cat into a psychotic frenzy, hissing, sputtering, clawing, and biting everything around itself trying to get away from the noise. The private was so frightened by the deranged kitty that she panicked and ran screaming out of the latrine and down the hall wearing nothing but the shampoo in her hair.

The alarm was of the type that got louder and louder and would not shut off until someone pushed the "Off" button. The louder the alarm got, the meaner the cat became. During the chaos that followed, we found it very easy to slip in and collect not only our guide-on and theirs, but also a few things out of their drill sergeant's office. During our escape, we paused only once as Private Maryweather rounded the corner. For a split second the world stopped, and I remembered her as the bombshell that had stepped out of the Camaro I had totaled. She apparently recognized me as well. She screamed something about costing her a fortune and landed a beautiful right hook square on my nose. She looked as though she wanted to do far more physical harm to me, but the sight of the other privates combined with her serious state of undress made her reconsider, and she continued on her panicked dash to safety. It was yet another thing that I wouldn't understand until later.

When we returned to our own barracks, I took it upon myself to report our victory to Drill Sergeant Bratton. I approached his office door, knocked twice, and waited to be called. Upon the command "Enter," I marched into his office and presented our prizes. Drill Sergeant Bratton was amazed that we had not only retrieved our own flag but had also managed to acquire several things that had been lying around in the C Company drill sergeant's office. Among the items we had stolen were the keys to their company van, their First Sergeant's duty uniform, their Senior Drill Sergeant's desk name plate, and the Commander's coffee cup. When I had finished my report, Drill Sergeant Bratton only had two questions for me: what had happened to my nose, and why didn't I grab their guide-on? My answer was straight forward and truthful…technically.

"Drill Sergeant, I had a run in with an old acquaintance.

And as for their guide-on, I didn't think it was in the best interest of the company for us to stoop to their level and bring it back to our barracks like they did to us. That would have been too predictable." Truthfully, we hadn't brought it back to the company. We had taken it up to base headquarters where the American Flag was flown daily and run it up that flagpole to be discovered by the base commander in the morning.

I mentioned earlier there were a few changes to several individuals' military careers. The three privates who had assisted me in the heist were not only taken off the "S" list, they were made squad leaders for their platoons, where they learned valuable leadership skills and earned promotion points toward their next rank. Sergeant Major Cat was stripped of his "rank" and delivered to the Humane Society in hopes of his finding a stress-free home. The female private who had gone streaking from the latrine washed out of the army and returned to being a secretary in the financial world just to get away from all the embarrassment. As for myself, I gained the confidence I needed to get through the rest of my training, although it didn't seem to help my luck. The morning after the heist, Drill Sergeant Bratton received a call from the base commander informing him that stunts like hanging a guide-on from the commander's flag pole would not be tolerated and that he should launch a full investigation and deal harshly with the individual responsible. Drill Sergeant Bratton, having known who was behind the raising of the flag, called me into his office and with a smile on his face sentenced me to two weeks of CQ duty.

True to his word, Drill Sergeant Bratton arranged my transfer into his platoon and, after the stress of trying to please Drill Sergeant Shining was off my shoulders, the weeks of training started to fly by. Before I knew it, we were all getting our dress uniforms out of our lockers and getting them ready for graduation. Wanting to look my best in my class A's, I took them to the post dry cleaners and had them cleaned, pressed, and starched. I also had them sew on a set of Sta-Brite® buttons so I wouldn't have to worry about ruining my uniform with the brass polish. I soon found out it wouldn't have made any difference.

On graduation day the air was electrified with anticipation of the upcoming ceremonies. Everyone in my class was anxious to transition from the training phase of their careers to their permanent unit assignments. We were the first people out of the barracks and while everyone else fell into formation, we partook in one of the graduation day traditions. We broke all the rules. Instead of wearing our PT uniforms, we were all dressed in white t-shirts, black shorts, mismatched socks, and flip-flops. It was the last chance for the drill sergeants to "smoke" us and the tradition was to give them a valid reason. The drill sergeants enjoyed this ritual as much as we did, inventing new and interesting ways for us to embarrass ourselves in front of the entire company. One such exercise was having us run around in a tight circle with our foreheads resting on a baseball bat until we were completely dizzy. When we were good and tipsy, we were told to do whatever random exercise the drill sergeant wanted us to do until we couldn't do any more due to exhaustion or until we were laughing too hard to move.

After our final round of corporal punishment, we were told to get cleaned up and report for inspection in our dress uniforms. With a bounce in our step we rushed up the stairs and into our rooms and in less than ten minutes we were all standing outside the drill sergeant's office. Unlike the inspection in basic training where we were punished for every little discrepancy on our uniforms, this one was fairly pleasant. Drill Sergeant Bratton slowly and methodically moved down the line of soon-to-be graduates and addressed all of the minor problems that he came across – a tie crooked here, a ribbon out of place there. When he was standing in front of me, I went to attention and awaited his verdict. The only thing he found amiss on my uniform was a string hanging from the button on my right breast pocket. He reached into his pocket and pulled out his lighter with the intent of burning it off. I learned two very important lessons that day: always inspect the sewing on any article that you have altered professionally, and heavily-starched woolen uniforms are extremely flammable. The flame seemed to leap off of his lighter and seek out my chest, setting the entire front of my uniform ablaze. The drill sergeant made a quick decision, grabbed a glass of ice water off of his desk, and doused the fire. Singed, soaked, and thinking that this was all par for the course, I made my way back up to my room to try and salvage my uniform in time for graduation. For the next hour and a half I worked on my jacket, first wiping off the soot from the burnt starch and then drying it with a heat gun we used to polish our boots, all the while being extremely careful not to reignite the remaining starch. With fifteen minutes to spare I made my way back down to the drill sergeant's office for inspection, having removed every trace of the arson.

The graduation ceremony was held in the small conference room in the back of the school house. At the rear of the room was a small stage made out of highly-polished oak and a matching podium. The steps up to the stage were very well worn from the countless soldiers who had graduated in previous years, and the stage looked as if it was coated in several hundred coats of floor wax. The floor directly in front of the podium had a very peculiar set of marks on it. There were two parallel streaks about twelve inches apart, approximately four inches wide and two feet long. My intense focus on the marks while trying to discern where they had come from made me nearly miss being called up on stage to receive my graduation letter and wings. I rose to my feet and calmly walked up onto the stage and stood before the podium. The instructor handed my certificate to me and then stepped aside for Drill Sergeant Bratton to pin my wings on my chest. Drill Sergeant Bratton placed my wings on my chest, drew back his fist and drove it into my chest with such force that I literally slid backward two feet, which satisfied my curiosity about the marks on the floor and officially completed my training.

Chapter 3
Present Day

Mr. Jonson pushed himself away from the desk. He was feeling terrible. Every joint in his body ached and he needed a rest. Martin was at his side in an instant.

"How are you feeling, Sir?"

"Not bad, considering that I'm as old as dirt and have been stuck in front of a computer for the last– "

Mr. Jonson doubled over into a coughing fit and grabbed onto Martin for support. Martin helped him over to the office couch and eased him down.

"Sir, you should really see a doctor about that cough. I have done everything I can for you and you have not improved at all."

David eyeballed his butler suspiciously, "If you can't do anything about my health issues, what makes you think that some hotshot doctor is going to be any better? Besides, it's just an annoying cough. It will go away on its own, you'll see."

"Mr. Jonson, in all my years of service I have seen too many people pass away because of sheer ignorance. You know as well as I do that it is not just a simple cough, and I am not going to stand around and let you kill yourself with stupidity. I am going to make you an appointment to see the doctor as soon as possible."

Martin left the room to make the call, and David forced himself to his feet to give chase. He felt sure that going to see the doctor wasn't necessary, and he was about to continue protesting when a very peculiar thing happened. The room appeared to slowly rotate around him on several different axes all at once. The next thing he knew, he was back on the couch with Martin leaning over him with an I-told-you-so look on his face.

When Martin was sure David was conscious, he went about the task of cleaning up the mess that Mr. Jonson had made of the end table when he had landed on it. After he had finished removing the debris, he went back out into the foyer to call the doctor's office.

The appointment was scheduled for four o'clock the following afternoon, and despite the intense grumbling, complaining, and belly-aching, Martin managed to deliver his elderly charge to the office on time.

"I still don't see why you think it's so important that I see the doctor, Martin. Despite the coughing, I feel quite good."

As soon as David finished speaking those words, another round of coughing racked his body. Martin just shook his head and excused himself in order to sign in with the receptionist.

Twenty minutes after Martin had signed in, a young nurse stepped into the waiting room and called for Mr. Jonson. Martin turned to offer his hand to assist David to his feet and was surprised to find him already up and making his way toward the nurse. When they were settled in the exam room and the nurse had excused herself, Martin gave his boss a questioning look.

"Sir, I hate to burst your bubble, but she is *way* too young for you and on top of that, she is married."

"Martin, getting the girl is no longer my primary goal. It's being able to give chase at all that helps me cope with my advanced age. The fact that I will never again be able to land a catch like that doesn't deter me from trying."

"Coping with your advanced age is exactly why we are

here. How do you think it would look if you dropped dead trying to catch up with some pretty young nurse?"

"I guess they could say I died chasing a dream," he said, grinning.

Their verbal sparring was brought to an abrupt halt when the door to the exam room opened, and the youngest doctor that either David or Martin had ever seen walked into the room.

"Doc, I believe you are younger than that TV doctor appeared to be. Does your mother know where you are?" David glanced at Martin and gave him a wink.

"Mr. Jonson, the young doctors are only allowed to practice on cadavers, those patients without insurance, and senile old men. Since you are not dead, you have Blue Cross, and I am still here, that leaves two possibilities: I'm not as young as you think I am, or you have a severe mental issue."

Martin made a coughing noise that sounded vaguely like the word "Several," which earned him a stern look from David and a chuckle from the doctor.

"Mr. Jonson, I do have a question about the paperwork you filled out. Where it asks for your date of birth you wrote June 30, 1980, which would make you just about eighty years old. Yet in the age slot you wrote eighty-five. So which is it?"

"Doc, I didn't come here to argue my age. The reason I came today is because Martin is concerned about my health even though I tell him it's nothing to worry ab–" David doubled over as another coughing fit racked his frail body, "–out. It's just an annoying cough that I can't seem to shake."

"That doesn't sound like any ordinary cough to me. I would like to run a few tests if you don't mind."

"Whatever you say, Doc."

Several hours later, after he had been poked, prodded, and examined more ways than anyone should have to endure,

David had had enough. He was just about to tell the doctor what he could do with his procedures when the doctor himself declared the exam complete.

"Well doc, what's the prognosis?"

"Your x-rays were inconclusive, and the rest of your test results won't be back for a week. So for now, I would recommend lots of rest and relaxation."

"Did you hear that, Martin? He said, 'Recommend.' "

"Yes, Sir, he did. He also said, 'Lots.' "

David glared at Martin, knowing full well that Martin would take the doctor's recommendation as a full prescription and force him to relax. The silence stretched on for a few minutes and when it had gone from awkward to uncomfortable, the doctor decided to dismiss his patient.

"Well, Mr. Jonson, as much as I would love to keep you here for more tests, I am sure that you and Martin have places you would rather be. I will give you a call when your test results arrive."

"Thanks Doc. Let's go home, Martin. You have some writing to do."

"As you wish, Sir."

Chapter 4
First Unit

"Well, Martin, where did we leave off?"

"Sir, are you sure that you are feeling up to this? You were getting pretty worked up last time."

"Just answer the question."

Martin brought up the file and read off the last sentence.

"One moment, Sir, 'Drill Sergeant Bratton placed my wings on my chest, drew back his fist and drove it into my chest with such force that I literally slid backward two feet, which satisfied my curiosity about the marks on the floor and officially completed my training.' I believe you were just about to move on to your first permanent duty station."

"That sounds about right. Let's start there."

With the training portion of my career completed, it was now time to move on to my assigned unit. Boarding the bus, I took one last look around the training billets and breathed a huge sigh of relief, hoping I would never have to see it again. I dropped myself into the first available seat and made myself comfortable; my destination was fourteen hours away.

Upon arrival at McEntire Air National Guard Station, I was met at the bus stop by my new platoon sergeant, SSG Noonan. My first reaction in the presence of a senior NCO was to go to parade rest and await orders. He just shook his head, mumbled something about being able to tell that I was fresh out of training, grabbed one of my bags, and asked if I wanted a lift to the barracks. I picked up my other bag and followed him to a white van that was parked nearby. After we had loaded my bags into the vehicle, he decided to give me a little advice.

"Private, around here we are quite a bit more relaxed than you are apparently used to. This isn't training; you don't have to go to parade rest every time an NCO walks by anymore. You'll still need to salute officers when you see them, unless you are on the flight line, and you are still required to be respectful to everyone, but you can tone it down a few notches."

I thanked him for the advice, and we climbed into the van.

Fifteen minutes later, we pulled up to the barracks that I would be calling home for the indeterminate future. As I retrieved my bags from the back, he handed me a key that had "3-B" engraved on it.

"Muster is at six o'clock in the morning in front of the armory. Be prepared to run a little ways. After PT is over, I will take you over to meet the high brass and get you squared away. For now just go get some rest, I will see you in the morning."

I thanked him and watched him as he drove off, wondering where exactly the armory was and how long it took to get there.

When I reached my room, I was met by a frazzled-looking individual who seemed rather put out to discover he was being assigned a new roommate. I told him I would request a different room if he had a problem with me staying there, but he dismissed the idea with a wave of his hand.

"It's not that I don't like you, you seem like a good person. I was just getting used to the idea of having the room to myself. I just got rid of my last good-for-nothing roommate not two days ago. My name is Todd, by the way, Todd Burchette."

After I had introduced myself and put my bags on my

bunk, my curiosity got the better of me, and I had to ask about his last roommate. Todd looked at me and took a deep breath, as if preparing himself for a long and painful story.

"A couple months ago, Private Milton was assigned to be my roommate because he couldn't get along with his previous roommate. It didn't take long to figure out why Milton and his last roommate fought a lot. Milton would leave trash all over the place and then blame me for it. He would leave his dirty dishes all over the room and refused to pick them up. And when it came time for a barracks inspection, he would leave for several hours so he wouldn't have to be involved with the clean up. When confronted with his shortcomings, he would become violent and start throwing stuff. Since nobody in my chain of command would do anything about it, I decided to take matters into my own hands.

"The last time he threw something it was a glass chess set of mine, which shattered against the wall. At that point I decided enough was enough so I threw him out the door, literally. Unfortunately, I forgot to open it first. I haven't seen Milton since."

I assured him that he wouldn't have any trouble out of me, and after a brief discussion about where we were both from, I went to bed to get some much needed rest.

The next few weeks seemed to fly by in a blur. I was constantly meeting new people in my chain of command and desperately trying to remember their names. Three weeks after arriving at my unit, I was finally introduced to the pilot I would be assigned to as his crew chief. Philippe Foullupe, aka Phil Foul-Up, was probably the best pilot in our unit. He had the reputation of someone who could take a brick, paint a tail number on it, and successfully make it fly a hover pattern around the airfield. Another reputation Phil had earned over

the years was one of an avid practical joker, and he loved it
when his crew chiefs would get in on the act. While on my
first check ride with him, I became the unlucky target of one
of his most famous practical jokes.

One of the various safety devices that a crew chief wears
is called a monkey harness. It is a full body harness that
attaches the crew member to the aircraft via a long lanyard.
This allows the crew member to move about the aircraft
while in flight with some sort of protection in case he or she
should happen to fall out. However, it can be used against its
wearer given the right circumstances.

My first check flight with Phil started out like every
flight I had done in school. I did all of the outside pre-flight
checks while the pilots got the engines spooled up. The crew
chief who was in charge of observing me was sitting in the
cabin chatting with the pilot as I approached to remove the
wheel chocks from under the aircraft. When I bent down
to pick them up, the crew chief reached out the window,
hooked a twenty-foot lanyard onto my monkey harness, and
slapped the pilot on the back of the head. The next thing I
knew, I was being lifted into the air dangling helplessly from
the end of the lanyard. Phil carried me all the way down the
flight line, in front of the hangers, and finally set me down
in the drainage pond at the end of the runway. To add insult
to injury, as soon as there was sufficient slack in the line the
crew chief unhooked it from the aircraft and then they all
flew off to complete their flight. Soggy, disoriented, and not
the least bit amused, I made my way back to the hanger.
Instead of changing out of my sodden flight suit, I
decided to get even with Phil while he was out flying around.
I went to my platoon sergeant and asked him what Mr.
Foullupe drove and where he parked his vehicle. Judging,

correctly, that I was out for revenge against a practical joker, he quietly informed me that it was a new ford pickup and that it was usually parked in the back corner of the parking lot. I thanked him and went to get some supplies.

Fifteen minutes later I had collected my materials and made my way out to the parking lot to find my intended target. In the very back corner of the lot, just as I was told, was a brand new red ford pickup. The first task I set before myself was jacking up the rear end of the truck. When I had the back tires a mere half inch off the ground, I slid a couple of cinder blocks under the axle and removed the jack. Next, I wrapped the entire drive shaft from end to end with large zip ties. The final touch was to jam a handful of gravel into the treads of the back tires. Satisfied that my practical joke prep work was complete, I made my way to the locker room to change into a dry uniform.

When the day finally came to an end, I made my way out to the parking lot to watch my vengeance unfold. I found a nice tree to sit under where I could observe the area and took a seat. A few minutes later SSG Noonan came out and asked me if I needed a ride back to the barracks.

"No thanks, Sergeant. I want to wait until Mr. Foullupe gets into his truck and tries to drive off. I want to see the look on his face when he finds out he's been had."

A puzzled look crossed SSG Noonan's face.

"Private, Mr. Foullupe went home about two hours ago."

I looked across the parking lot at the pickup I had vandalized and I noticed the sticker on the windshield denoting the rank of the owner. Two stars, indicating the rank of Major General. Mr. Foullupe was a Chief Warrant Officer and would have had a sticker with two *dots*. I shot an accusing glance at my platoon sergeant.

"I thought you said it was the new ford pickup at the back of the lot!"

SSG Noonan just shook his head and chuckled. "I said the *blue* ford pickup… Wait a sec, what *new* ford pickup did you sabotage?"

"The red one over there…"

I started toward the truck to reverse the damage I had caused, but my platoon sergeant caught my arm.

"It's too late to try and fix it now. The General will be coming out of his office any minute and you don't want to be caught doing anything to his truck. Besides, if we just leave without drawing attention to ourselves, he just might think that it was Mr. Foullupe messing with him. Get in the car and I will take you back to the barracks."

The following morning, a formation was held in front of the main hanger and rumors of promotions spread throughout the ranks. Of course I had no such delusions; I knew exactly why the formation was called. As I stood at attention, my mind kept flashing back to the previous day, trying to figure out who had seen me and ratted me out to the General after I sabotaged his truck. I was so caught up in thoughts of my impending punishment that I hadn't heard anything our commander said during his speech. When the General stepped up to the podium in front of the formation with a folder in his hand, my blood started to run cold in my veins and a ghostly image of a blue and white sports car tumbling down the road flashed before my eyes.

The General barked a simple command that I just couldn't will myself to disobey, "Private Jonson! Front and Center!"

As I made my way up to the front of the formation, I could feel every accusing stare bore into me. It felt as if everyone in the company knew what I had done and none of them saw the humor in it. When I reported to the General and completed my salute he grabbed onto my lapel and ripped off the rank that was on my collar. I had suspected demotion at the very least for my crimes and stood fast, awaiting the rest of my punishment.

To my complete and total amazement, the General shook my hand and said to me, "Congratulations, *Specialist* Jonson. Keep up the good work."

I was utterly speechless. Looking down at my lapel, I noticed the brand new specialist rank that was pinned where my private first class rank had been. I managed to choke out a thank you and made my way back to the formation as the next name on the list was called. I didn't have the guts to tell the man who had just promoted me that I was the one who had done all those terrible things to his truck.

With new rank came new responsibilities and different details that had to be seen to. I worked hard and neither my platoon sergeant nor I ever told anyone about the general's truck. After a few years, I finally worked my way up the promotion list again and was ready to receive my sergeant stripes. I was no longer going to be the peon who was forced to do all the menial work. I wanted to be the person doing the forcing. On the other hand, I would also be the person who received the blame if anything went wrong, and I was about to find out how wrong things could possibly go.

Two weeks before I was to receive my promotion, I was assigned the task of recovering a vehicle that had become stuck in a large mud hole on the back side of the base. When I asked what kind of vehicle we were recovering, I was told I would find out when I got there, and I would have seven eager privates and two humvees at my disposal. We loaded one of the humvees up with all of the recovery straps we were going to need, piled into the vehicles, and made our way out to the mud hole.

The vehicle in question was a military police pickup. Neither the sergeant driving the truck nor the lieutenant in the passenger seat could give me a good reason as to why they were in the mud in the first place. Noticing that their vehicle had its own set of recovery hooks located under the bumper, I sent out one of the privates to hook up a tow strap. The private grumbled a bit but nevertheless dove in and attached a strap. Unfortunately, the strap wasn't long enough to reach the back of our hummer, so instead of sending him back out into the mud, I had another private attach a second strap to the first using a small shackle. The second strap was then attached to the back of the hummer, and we proceeded to pull out the stranded pickup.

Had I gone behind the second private and inspected the connection he made with the shackle, I could have avoided a major headache later, but hindsight is 20/20.

After all the connections were made, I jumped into the driver's seat and eased forward just enough to take the slack out of the straps. As soon as everyone was ready, I shifted into low gear and punched it, hoping that their pickup would just pop out of the mud fairly easily. But, because I hadn't checked the connection, the only thing that popped out was the pin from the shackle. The shackle snapped back at the pickup and smashed a neat hole in the center of the windshield. The sergeant behind the wheel decided he didn't want to be inside his truck anymore, jumped out, and promptly sank up to his waist in the mud. In order to extract the stranded NCO, the rest of the detail, including myself, dove into the mud and made a human chain and pulled him out. Thankfully, our second attempt at extricating the truck was successful, and we avoided breaking any more equipment in the process.

Being the kind of caring individ–

"Sir, if I may point out, you were NOT very kind to those

Military Police Officers. I seem to recall you telling the story a bit differently, with quite a few references to their– how did you put it– 'diminutive intelligence quotients.' "

"I made no such references. I had nothing except praise and encouraging comments for those fine officers. As a matter of fact…Martin, don't look at me that way."

"Sir, if you were as kind and caring as you would have your readers believe, how are you going to explain being arrested soon after extracting their vehicle?"

"I was a victim of police profiling."

"If you say so, Sir. I am sure they were arresting all foul-mouthed, slandering individuals who happened to be near the mud pit that day."

"They didn't arrest me for being foul-mouthed or for slander or even for destruction of government property. They arrested me because the lieutenant couldn't take a joke."

"That was some joke, Sir. If I recall the story correctly, the actual charges were for assault and battery."

"We will just have to let the readers decide on my innocence."

"As you wish, Sir."

After we had extracted their vehicle from the mud, the lieutenant heaved a huge sigh of relief and thanked us for keeping him out of that mess and ruining his uniform. I looked around at everyone who had helped me pull the truck out, including the sergeant who had put it there in the first place, and realized that the lieutenant was the only one of us who hadn't touched the mud. So I decided to correct the situation. I scooped up the spotless officer, carried him out into the pit, and plopped him face first into the mud. It wasn't until I had made it back to dry land that I realized I was the only one laughing–that is until the lieutenant retrieved his handcuffs from the truck.

The stockade at the MP station was very similar to what you might find at your local police station; bad food, bad company, and hard benches. It was three hours before anyone came to release me from my incarceration. Unfortunately my first sergeant took it upon himself to come and collect me. The look on his face when they opened the cell door brought back that familiar nauseous feeling and I could have sworn I heard a car crash in the distance.

Once he had secured my release and we started to drive away, he gave me one of those I-can't-believe-you-just-did-that looks and began to chuckle.

"Jonson, I don't know what came over you today, and quite frankly I can't make up my mind what to do about it. At the very least you can forget about your promotion. As you can probably guess, the old man wants your head on a platter and your rank on his desk. On the other hand, I have an off-the-record and completely unofficial thank you from the first sergeant of the MP battalion for taking that, how did he put it, 'Pompous, butt-kissing, know-it-all lieutenant' down a peg or two. His unofficial thanks also came with a pardon for smashing his windshield. He wrote that one off as equipment failure. So I will leave the choice up to you. Do you want to take a company grade article fifteen, which will probably strip a stripe off your collar, or, would you rather take door number two?"

I thought about my options for a few minutes and decided that anything would be better than going in front of the commander. How the first sergeant was able to get away with calling the major "old man" was beyond me. In the few short years I had been with the company, I had seen at least sixteen individuals lose rank to the major. I believe the major actually enjoyed demoting people and went as far as hanging their rank insignia on his bulletin board like so many trophy animal pelts, and I was determined not to let my hard-earned rank join his collection.

"What's door number two?"

The first sergeant just looked at me and grinned.

Chapter 5
Marching Orders

Two days and over six thousand miles later I staggered out into the blistering summer sun of northern Iraq. Door number two was a one year deployment with a small support group to an air base known as Camp Anaconda. At first I thought it wouldn't be so bad. Then the oppressive wall of heat hit me. That's when I learned that the soles of your boots will melt on the flight-line in one hundred forty degree heat. I quickly revised my opinion of my situation to something a little more appropriate and followed my comrades to our designated hanger.

"If I may ask, Sir, what exactly was your opinion of Iraq?"

"At the time? Hot, dusty, desolate, and definitely not worth spending a year there just to save a stripe on my collar. In hindsight however, I wouldn't trade my experience there for anything."

The hanger we were assigned to was massive. Commonly referred to as a HAS (pronounced haws), or Hardened Aircraft Shelter, it was originally tasked to house the Iraqi Air Force's Migs until our forces came in and took up residence. In each of its two enormous bays it held four Blackhawk helicopters, one of which was going to be mine for the next eleven months, twenty-eight days, fifteen hours and thirty-two minutes…. But who was counting.

As we approached the hanger entrance, my attention was drawn to a group of young privates attempting to erect a water tower next to the hanger. The tank they were lifting looked like it would hold about three thousand gallons, and judging by the water sloshing out the top, it was full. As the tank was lifted up, the private directing the crane stepped under the tank in order to better see the mount points on top of the tower. The world slowed down around me when I heard the sound of tearing fabric and realized that the two flimsy straps they had holding the tank were not going to hold any longer. I dropped all of my gear and took off at a sprint, and for that instant I forgot all about the oppressive heat, the glaring sun, the continuous countdown until my deployment was up, and any shred of self-preservation. All I was thinking about was getting that private out from under the tank before it fell. I let out a scream just before I got to the endangered individual and executed a tackle that any NFL defensive coach would be proud of, launching both of us clear of the tank.

You know those scenes in most action movies where the hero saves someone just in the nick of time and whatever was coming hits just behind their heels? Well this wasn't one of those scenes. Not only was the tank still in the air, but the private wasn't actually a private. She was a lieutenant. A very angry lieutenant. She slowly pulled herself up off the ground, grabbed me by the front of my uniform, drew back her fist, and was just about to show me how angry she was when the straps finally let go and the tank crashed down exactly where she had been standing. Several emotions crossed her face, anger, fear, astonishment, and finally gratitude. She thanked me profusely and asked me to accompany her to the commanders office to fill out an incident report. When I didn't move to follow her, she made her request again, this time as an order.

"I'm sorry, ma'am, but I don't think I can do that."

She started to regain some of the scarlet color that had just recently left her face and assumed the stance of someone who was used to people jumping when she said jump.

"Give me one good reason why you can't follow me."

"First of all ma'am, I have yet to report to my commander –"

"We can do that on the way."

"Second, my stuff is scattered all over the flight-line –"

"I will send some of my detail to pick up your stuff."

"And I think the tank landed on the heels of my boots."

She looked at my feet and, sure enough, one of the mount brackets welded to the tank had managed to drive itself through the backs of both of my boots, without touching my feet, and had effectively pinned the soles of the boots to the sand. With a chuckle she ordered her detail to help free my feet, and we were soon on our way to her commander's office.

Her commander's office was nothing more than a large field tent set up behind the hanger. As we approached his tent, I noticed that it was built inside the track that the huge hanger blast door used to run on. I asked the lieutenant if they ever worried about the doors crashing into the commander's tent.

"Nope. Those doors haven't worked since we got here. If we need them moved, we push them with one of our humvees. With all the rockets and stuff coming in, we just leave them closed anyway, so we really have no reason to fix them."

When we stepped into the tent, I was surprised at what they had done to the interior. The floor had been built up and a hardwood floor installed. A wall had been built out of plywood in the middle of the tent, dividing what appeared to be a makeshift mail room from the commander's office. The office door even had a small brass plaque displaying the commander's name and rank. Colonel Masters was at his desk looking over some paperwork.

The lieutenant knocked on the door.

"Sir, I don't know if you heard all the commotion or not, but we just had an incident with the water tank detail, and this specialist and I have come to make a report."

The colonel peered over his glasses at the lieutenant and smirked, "This wouldn't have anything to do with those straps that I told you wouldn't hold the weight you were planning on hoisting, would it?"

The lieutenant sighed, "You would be correct, Sir. The straps didn't hold up. If it hadn't been for this specialist here, I would be a whole lot shorter now."

"Is that so?" Masters directed his gaze over to me, "I guess I owe you a debt of gratitude. Tell me, Son, what's your name and who is your commander?"

I took out my orders and found the name of my commander. I looked at the colonel and smiled.

"Sir, would you happen to be Colonel *William* Masters of the one hundred fifty-first aviation battalion?"

"Yes, that's my name. Let me guess, you are Specialist David Jonson from Det One Lima company. First Sergeant Rudderick told me you would be coming. Told me you were anxious to get noticed and make a name for yourself. Also said that you were trying to work off a bit of bad karma. Well, I would say that saving the life of your platoon leader is a good way to get noticed. Your paper work looks to be in order, except for one thing. It says here that your rank is that of specialist. I don't agree with that. You look more like a sergeant to me. Here, pin these on your collar. Oh, and by the way, welcome to Bravo Company, home of the Flying Bulldogs."

Later that day I was introduced to my first real experience of hostile fire. I was standing outside our hanger getting to know my flight crew when an enemy mortar round flew overhead. Instead of everyone running for the hanger or any of the number of small bunkers that were placed about, people started placing bets where the round would hit and how many more rounds would come in. I was completely flabbergasted. Here I was getting ready to run, screaming for cover, and everyone else was pulling out their wallets and placing bets. After ten minutes without anymore incoming rounds, the all clear was sounded and all bets were settled. The biggest winner just happened to be my platoon leader. She walked over to me and handed me half of her winnings.

"Here, if it wasn't for you, I wouldn't have been around to place any bets."

One of my pilots leaned over to me as she walked away and said, "I hope you bring us as much luck as you have brought her. Our last crew chief didn't have much at all in the way of luck. His first flight out he took a 7.62 round through the right shoulder and one in the leg. He's now at home with his arm stuck in a sling and a bad limp."

I paled a little at the realization that I had been sent to replace one of this company's casualties and said a little prayer that no one would have to be sent to replace me due to the same circumstances.

For the first few months my luck seemed to hold out and we had all relaxed into a routine: meet for breakfast, review our daily mission log, pre-flight the aircraft, fly our missions, and end the day over dinner at the chow hall. The morning of day seventy-five, our routine was changed by my platoon leader. We were ordered to transport a group of special forces guys to a location that would be disclosed upon takeoff. As we lifted off, the commander of the task force called up to the pilot and told him to head northeast as low and fast as we could go. The pilot just shrugged and nosed the aircraft over, starting what was to become my last flight in country.

Our next course correction came when we overflew a small river. Once again we were ordered to fly as low and fast as we could, but now we were to follow the river north. The pilot acknowledged the order and banked the aircraft over. Almost as soon as we were over the river, we were attacked by the locals. Not the gun toting guys that we were trained to take on, but the large feathered variety. About thirty birds, very similar to geese, lifted off in a magnificent display of grace and beauty, straight into our flightpath. Feathers, guts and bird dropping seemed to explode out of every opening on our aircraft. All of the windshields were smashed in and some of the birds even survived long enough to make it to the back of the cabin area where the special forces guys were strapped in. All those tough guys with their smile-in-the-face-of-death attitudes started screaming like a room full of ten year old girls and leaped from the crippled aircraft into the waters below. The last commando out the door paused just long enough to thank us for the ride and inform us that they would find alternate transportation.

The copilot started looking for a good place to set down the aircraft, and I started scanning the surrounding areas looking for anything that might be a threat to a downed –

"Sir, I do not remember you ever telling me that you crash-landed during your tour of duty."

"That's because we didn't, Martin. Our pilot said that he wasn't walking back to the base and he certainly wasn't waiting for someone to come pick him up. He flew us all the way back and earned us all the broken wing award and a silver star for himself."

Chapter 6
Luck Changes

With our aircraft out of commission for a while, I found myself with a lot of free time on my hands. After the third day, I started to explore the hanger we were assigned to. One of the things that had intrigued me was the massive set of doors at either end of the hanger. I had never seen anyone attempt to operate the doors, so I flagged down the first sergeant and asked him about them.

"Well, Sergeant, when we first arrived in country, nobody could figure out how to work 'em. You are more than welcome to try and figure them out if its eating you up inside, just be careful."

"Thanks, Top."

I walked over to the set of doors at the back of the hanger and started looking them over. The doors were massive. Each door weighed at least fifteen to twenty tons and had a hydraulically actuated lock pin made of solid steel. Upon closer inspection, I found a large wheel that appeared to be driven by a hydraulic motor which in turn was powered by an enormous accumulator. Stashed in a hidden compartment near the motor was a pump handle, several levers, and a single pressure gauge. On the inside of the door to the compartment was a schematic and a list of warnings, which of course were written in Arabic. Abandoning any hope of deciphering the diagram on the door I resorted to what any insanely curious and carefree individual would do. I started pushing and pulling each of the levers to see if anything happened. When nothing happened, I turned to the pump and pressure gauge. I pumped the handle for what seemed like an eternity until the needle had moved about three quarters of its travel around the face of the gauge and started pulling on the levers one by one. This time, when I pulled the first lever I heard the locking pin retract into its housing. Excited with my progress, I moved on to the second lever and yanked down on it anticipating the door to move. Much to my disappointment, I heard the locking pin slide back down into the notch in the floor, and the pressure gauge bottomed out. I pumped the pressure back up, this time making the needle on the gauge spin all the way around before stopping. Once again I pulled the first lever and was rewarded with the sound of the locking pin retracting. I skipped over the second lever and pulled the third. Had I been able to read the Arabic warnings on the schematic and the pressure readings on the gauge, I would have known not to try and operate the door over a certain pressure. When I pulled the third lever, the pressure was well over the recommended operating levels for the drive, and the door flew open with unbelievable force and didn't stop when the controls were pulled from my hand. Nor did it stop when it smashed into the commander's tent. Thankfully, the commander wasn't in the tent at the time, but that didn't make him any less angry when he came back and found it and all of his belongings crushed by a door that supposedly wasn't capable of being moved without a large vehicle pushing it.

Shaking with fury, the commander walked over to me and proceeded to remove the sergeant stripes from my collar. He then ordered me to report directly to the duty officer for poop duty where I was to serve out the remainder of my time in country. Which, looking on the bright side, was only another one hundred seventy-six days, sixteen hours, and two minutes. But again, who was counting.

Poop duty was exactly that. All the human waste on the base was pumped into large trucks and brought to a single location where it was mixed with diesel fuel and burned in large drums until all that was left was a bunch of ashes. The ashes were then buried in large pits dug by the people unfortunate enough to get assigned to the poop detail. For five hours a day I would dig pits. I would then be allowed to rest for an hour while the ashes were dumped in, and then I would have to fill the pits back in with dirt. Any leftover soil when the pit was filled was then shoveled into sandbags for use all over the base.

While digging my hundredth or so poop ash pit, I started talking to myself, saying things like, "When I think my life has finally hit bottom, they give me a shovel." About four feet into the pit I made a discovery that forever changed my life. My shovel struck something metallic and I thought I heard someone howl in pain. Dropping to my knees, I started digging around a small shape in the soil and quickly unearthed a golden sphere. As I held it in my hands I noticed some odd-looking engravings all over it. Looking around to see if I was being watched, I quickly slipped the softball-sized artifact into one of my cargo pockets and finished digging the hole.

After my daily punishment was complete, I made my way back to my room, which I shared with one other enlisted soldier from my company. The room was small, only ten by ten with just enough room for two single beds, two wall lockers, and one small table we had built when I first moved in. Thankfully, we were on opposite shifts, so I basically had the room to myself. As I entered the room, I removed the orb from my pocket, set it on the table, and started tossing my gear onto my bed. The last piece of equipment that I took off was my thigh holster along with my service automatic. While removing my holster, I bumped into the table which caused the orb to roll off and strike the floor.

"Ouch! That is twice you have struck me, and I will no

longer stand for it!"

I drew my pistol, clicked the safety off, and frantically looked around for the source of the complaint. My fear quickly dissolved into confusion when I confirmed that I was the only one in the room. While returning my sidearm to its holster, I verbally expressed my apparent loss of mental stability.

"Just because you are hearing voices does not mean you are going, as you say, 'nuts.' "

Contrary to the reassurances from the disembodied voice, I could feel my sanity slipping away.

"OK, Voice, or whatever you are, if I'm not out of my mind, would you please explain yourself and how I can hear you and not see you?"

"Look down."

I slowly looked to the floor expecting to see a small, talking rodent of some sort confirming my fading sanity, but the only thing on the floor –besides my boots and some of my roommates dirty clothes –was the orb that I had dug up and smuggled back in my pocket.

"I get it, Voice. You must be my conscience speaking to me through a mental breakdown due to heat exhaustion. You win, I will take the orb ba –"

"I believe you have the wrong idea. I am not your conscience, nor am I an hallucination brought on by heat exhaustion. The voice you are hearing, my voice, is coming from the golden object at your feet, and I would appreciate it if you would quit being so careless with me."

I bent over, retrieved it from the floor, and started rubbing the dirt off in an attempt to decipher the markings on it and find some sort of speaker, while still doubting my mental stability.

"Oh, that feels wonderful! I have not been rubbed like that in... Why did you stop?"

I stared at the orb in disbelief. With most of the dirt and grime removed, I could start to see what the markings truly were. Not all the markings were a language as I had thought before but were the outlines of the seven continents along with country borders. The only writing on the globe was five small words, written across the north pole, that seemed to change depending on where I placed my right thumb. As my thumb passed over Germany, the words changed to, *Lass mich dein Führer sein*. Sliding my thumb over to France, the words shifted to, *Laissez-moi être votre guide*. The words shifted and morphed through the languages until I stopped on the United States. Standing out in English were the following words: *Let me be your guide*.

I sat down on my bunk and decided that so long as I was going to go down the rabbit hole...

"Wha.. What... What are you?"

"I am what is left of what you would call a genie. Complete with the lamp, the smoke, and the famous phrase, 'How may I serve you, Master?' Now I am nothing more than a mystical travel agent."

"Travel agent? Are you some kind of interactive map?"

"I will have you know that I am more than just a map, my friend. Here let me show you. Pick a location, any location, use your right index finger, touch it on the map and say, 'I want to go there.' "

Not knowing what to think, I picked a spot at random, touched it, and said the mantra. With a burst of white light, I was standing in the middle of a field surrounded by a large herd of cattle. Looking down at the globe, my finger was on the northwestern United States. A small red dot appeared in the country of Iraq and a blue circle appeared around the tip of my finger and slowly contracted down to a single blue point. I looked around, completely dumbfounded. Off in the distance, I could see a large sign next to a busy highway. I walked toward the sign hoping to get some idea of where I was. The large print on the sign read, "Welcome to Billings, Montana."

"Well, Globe or Genie or whatever you want me to call you, you have made a believer out of me. Now how do I get back?"

"First of all, you may call me whatever you wish, since you found me and have now used my powers, you are officially my master until you are dead or you voluntarily give me up. Second –"

"Wait a sec. What do you mean by that? Dead or I voluntarily give you up? Nobody else can use your powers?"

"To everyone else I am just a golden globe. If you give me away, then you will no longer be able to hear my voice or use my powers. If you lose me or I am stolen, then nobody will be able to use my powers until you are dead."

"Right, so they have to kill me to be able to use your powers. I think I will just keep that information to myself. So how do I get back to where I came from?"

"Just touch the red dot on the map that indicates where you started and say, 'I want to go back,' and it will be so."

I touched the dot, said the words, and with a flash of light I was back in my room in Iraq. I sat back down on my bunk and a million questions began flooding my mind.

"Until we can agree on a good name for you I'll just call you Genie. Now what I want to know is, how did you get into this predicament?"

"To which predicament are you referring, Master? The one that enslaved me in a life of servitude as a genie? Or the one that stripped me of my powers?"

"Um, both I guess."

"Well, Master, it is a –"

"You're not going to call me Master all the time are you?"

"What would you have me call you, Master?"

"My name is David Jonson. You can call me David, or you can simply address me as Sir."

"As you wish, Sir."

"Now, go ahead and tell me how you came to be as you are now."

"Well, Sir, it is a very long story, but if you insist...."

Chapter 7
How He Began

"Many thousands of years ago, before the fall of man, I was in the service of the Lord as one of His angels. Just after the fall, I became sympathetic to man's afflictions and made it my task to alleviate some of their suffering, but the Lord rebuked me, telling me that man should learn on his own to survive in his new environment. He told me that if I were to provide everything for man without teaching him, he would be as a babe and need to be constantly provided for.

"At the time, I had not seen the wisdom in His words, nor did I agree with His actions. On one particularly cold night I took it upon myself to provide a fire for Adam and Eve to warm themselves by. The night was not so cold that they would have been in any sort of danger, they just looked uncomfortable, so I appeared before them in all my splendor, announced that my name was Prometheus, set a log on fire with a snap of my fingers, and returned to my post. That night I learned why man needed to learn on his own. The first thing Adam did was try to pick up the flaming log to bring it over to Eve. As you can imagine, he did not hold it for long and when he dropped it, it rolled down the hill into some dry brush and started the first large-scale forest fire, consuming several thousand acres of forest.

"The punishment for my disobedience was to serve man just as I had before, only I would not have any choice in how or when. I was bound to the metal of a golden lamp and whoever controlled the lamp would control my powers, with four exceptions. First, I could not kill anyone, nor could I bring anyone back from the dead. I could not grant immortality and, lastly, I could not make anyone fall in love.

"The first few hundred years of my imprisonment were spent hidden in the middle of the charred remains of the forest I had burned down. The first person to venture out and find my golden prison was a young man who, frankly, did not have any business controlling my powers. The first thing the young man wished for was the ability to fly. As per my punishment I was not allowed to do anything except follow my master's wishes to the letter. The young man lifted off the ground and took to the skies. He actually did fairly well until he tried to fly through a tree. The only thing I could do was engrave the warning 'be careful what you wish for' on a nearby stump before I was once again sucked back into the lamp to wait for my next master.

"And so it went for thousands of years. Someone would find me and use my powers for a short while. Those who did not kill themselves in some way would eventually ruin their lives trying to find happiness in material things. That is, until I was discovered by a man named Borjigin Temüjin in the year 1188.

"Master Borjigin was the most paranoid master I had ever served. The reason he was so paranoid was because everyone he knew was out to get him in some way or other. When he was only ten years old his brother attacked him during a hunting trip and he was forced to kill him in self defense. At the time he discovered my lamp, he was twenty-five years old and being held captive by some of his father's old allies.

"The first wish he made was for eloquence and with that simple wish he changed the course of history. Only one year after I had made his acquaintance, Master Borjigin had become a general over the army of the very men who had held him captive. As he surveyed his troops, he wished for his men to be the best fighting force in the world and for the military knowledge to lead them successfully. Bound as I was, I had no choice but to grant his wish.

"By the year 1206, he had started to carve an empire out of Asia the likes of which had never been seen and had changed his name to Genghis Khan. For the next twenty years of his life, until his sixty-fifth birthday, he used my powers along with his generals to expand his borders further and further. It was at that time that he decided he no longer needed my services and did not want me to fall into the hands of anyone who would potentially oppose him. He ordered my lamp to be melted down, believing the process would destroy me and my powers. When my lamp was melted down, the blacksmith used the gold to cast several objects to honor Khan's rise to power.

"The first object cast was a ring to represent the unity of the people. Since he had unified the people through a common language, and the ring retained a small part of my power, anyone who wore the ring was given the power to speak and understand any language. The second object was a dragon to represent his fierceness in battle and military leadership. Just like the ring, it retained a small portion of my power and gave its possessor confidence, strength, and courage as well as the absolute authority to lead, which nobody could resist. The third item was a small golden Buddha to signify the peace he brought to the Mongol people. It subsequently brought peace to whoever was in its sphere of influence. The fourth item, a delicate necklace, was actually made to honor his wife and her beauty. With the power of the necklace, the wearer became irresistibly beautiful. The fifth item, the one you found, was a globe to represent the entire world under Khan's rule. Since the globe was the biggest piece of the lamp, it is where my personality resides, and it gives the person who wields it the power to move, not only anywhere on earth but also through time as well."

I stopped the genie before he could continue and pointed out a flaw in his story. "How would the Mongols have known that the world was round? Why would he cast a globe, and not a plate map?"

The globe vibrated for a moment before answering, "In the early years of Khan's rule, we would sit and have discussions about strategy and the expansion of his empire. During one such discussion, Khan asked me what lay beyond the edges of the earth. It was at that time that I explained that the world was round. When he asked for proof, I took him up above the clouds and we circumnavigated the globe."

"All right, I'll buy that. What happened next?"

"When the items were presented and it was discovered that they still retained some powers, Khan ordered his most trusted servant to use the power of the globe to hide the other objects throughout the world so that none of his rivals could use them to take over his empire. His servant decided, on his own, to take it one step further and traveled through time as well to more completely hide them.

"The dragon was taken forward in time and presented to Emperor YongLe, who had rebuilt and changed the name of the Imperial City to The Forbidden City. The Buddha was actually given to a man named Gautama Siddhartha, somewhere south of the Himalayan Mountains in eastern India during the sixth century B.C. Every time the servant hid a piece, I could feel my powers growing weaker and weaker, which in turn made my accuracy during transport worse and worse. When he ordered me to take him to an island off the western coast of what would become England at a date of my choosing, I missed the island by about twenty miles and landed him in the water about a mile from the mainland. A local fisherman found him floundering in the water and rescued him. The servant gave the man the necklace as a token of appreciation for saving his life. Lastly, the ring was taken back in time to an ancient city in the land of Shinar and was hidden in the tunnels under a tower that was being built there.

"Upon the servant's return to Khan's palace, he presented Khan with the globe and tried to tell him his task was complete, but the only thing to come out of his mouth was gibberish. Khan placed the globe into a small wooden box and tried to make sense of what his servant was trying to say. He quickly became convinced that his servant had lost his mind and with one swift movement ran the servant through with his sword. He then ordered four of his guards to take the body along with the wooden box to the far west and bury them in the wasteland, far beyond the borders of the empire. And that is where you found me."

I sat on my bed deep in thought. Being able to go anywhere with just a simple command was amazing enough, but to find out that the genie had the ability to travel through time as well was almost unthinkable. Before I could decide on a course of action I had to have more information.

"Genie, you said as the servant hid the other items you lost power. What did you mean by that?"

"When I was first bound to the lamp, I could do anything that was asked of me, within the four rules. When the lamp was melted down and cast into the different artifacts, the shapes that were cast, the amount of gold used, and the symbolism of each item dictated the extent of their powers. When all the pieces were together I still had the focus, if not the ability, that I had when the lamp was whole. As the pieces were hidden, I could feel that focus slipping away. The most noticeable effect was the drop in accuracy when transporting someone into an area they had not transported to before."

"What do you mean by loss of accuracy?"

"With all of the other artifacts I could jump someone onto a small boat in the middle of the Pacific Ocean as long as the person I was transporting had an idea of about where it was. Now all I can do is promise to get within thirty miles of the target location."

"What about the time travel option? How does that work?"

"Turn the globe over. Do you see the five rings in Antarctica that look like latitudinal lines and the string of numbers on the South Pole? The numbers represent the target date and time that you wish to visit. If you read it left to right you would read year, month, day, hour, minute. If you take your left index finger and trace the outermost circle counterclockwise you will see the year count down. The second circle changes the month and so on. When you have the target date of your choice, all you need to do is use your right index finger to select a target area and say, 'I want to be there.' "

"Wait a second, I thought the globe was cast in 1226? The Mongols wouldn't have used this format to track time. This looks like the modern version of the Roman calendar."

"As with the inscription on the North Pole, the date format changes with the master. If you would like, I could change the format to whatever you prefer."

"I think this will do. What about going forward in time? Can I go forward and see my future?"

"You can go forward; however, any knowledge of the future that is brought to the present will change that future. So in essence you could not go into the *true* future at all. The reverse is also true, so be forewarned, any knowledge of the present that is taken to the past will change the present. Maybe not drastically, but it will change, and when you return to the present you may not like what you find. As for going into the future to see yourself, you could never find yourself, for you would have been missing since the moment you left the timeline to travel forward. You could theoretically go back and see a younger version of yourself; however, the dangers of time travel should not be taken lightly. For example, if you went back to the time of your conception and you caused a disturbance in your parent's household, you would cease to exist. You wouldn't disappear immediately; you would continue to exist in the past until you tried to travel through time again."

"Right, so if I do use it, use it carefully. Got it. Well, now what do I do? I can't just hand you over to the authorities. Who knows what would happen to you, and I can't very well put you back where I found you, can I? Just imagine if someone who really meant to do some harm got hold of you and had your powers at their disposal. What would you do if our roles were reversed?"

"Well, if you are so keen on not letting anyone else gain control of my powers, you have only three options. Option one: keep the globe hidden and never use it. Using it may draw attention to yourself and if you are trying to keep it a secret that is the last thing you want. Option two: attempt to destroy it. Personally I am against that option, but it is available. Lastly, you could try to reassemble the lamp. Doing so would give you control of my full powers as a genie and not just as a travel guide. You could use those powers to hide the lamp and my powers forever, or you could use them to free me from this golden prison. The last option is, of course, my preference."

I stared at the floor for a few minutes composing my thoughts. Destroying the globe was not an option, and I doubted my ability to keep it a secret, let alone resist the urge to use it. Option three did, in fact, seem like the best choice.

"Okay Genie, if I were to try and reassemble your lamp, where would I start?"

"First of all, you need to find the pieces. And it may not be as simple as going back to the time and place where they were hidden. Most, if not all of the artifacts, have probably been found and exploited throughout history, and to just remove them from the timeline could have disastrous results."

"Assuming that I can find all the pieces, how do I go about reassembling the lamp?"

"When you have all the pieces in your possession, you will have to find someone with the skills and the equipment to melt all of the pieces and cast them into a solid object. The shape will not matter much as long as you have all of the pieces, so it does not have to be in the shape of a lamp."

"And how would I go about freeing you? Is there some kind of magical incantation?"

"No, all you have to do is wish it and it will be so. But first we have to find all the pieces."

"I guess we have some research to do."

Chapter 8
Present Day

The phone rang and David started to get up to answer it, but before he could get on his feet, Martin had already answered the phone and was motioning for his boss to sit back down. Had the last few hours of dictating not taken so much out of him, he might have been more apt to argue; instead, he settled for grumbling under his breath and listening to Martin on the phone as he settled back into the couch.

"Yes, doctor... No, Sir, I have not let him off the couch... No, Sir, he has not eaten much now that you mention it... I understand... We would be more than happy to come back for more tests tomorrow... Ah, I see. Well, we shall be there straight away then. Thank you, Sir. Good bye."

"Well, Martin? Are you going to tell me or am I going to have to call the good doctor back and question him?"

"If you would rather talk to the doctor, Sir, you can do so in person as soon as we get there. He has asked us to come in as soon as we can."

"And you told him we were on our way without even asking me if I had any plans this afternoon. I guess I will just have to tell that young lady–"

"Sir, the last 'young lady' you had any interaction with was selling Girl Scout cookies and that was over two years ago. You scared her so badly when you answered the door that I had to write a formal letter of apology to her troop and explain to them that you were just kidding when you asked her if the cookies were made with real girl scouts. Though they did accept the apology, you were still blacklisted from all Girl Scout routes."

"Let's just get this over with. Bring the car around."

"As you wish, Sir."

An hour later, David and Martin were once again sitting in the exam room waiting for the doctor.

"Martin, weren't we just here yesterday?"

"No, Sir. It has been three days, but given your advanced age, I am surprised that you can remember being here at all."

"Listen, Pot, you're no spring chicken yourself. I mean you are at least–"

The door to the exam room opened and the doctor strolled in looking at the chart he was carrying. He pulled up a chair and cleared his throat.

"Mr. Jonson, your test results have come in and I'm not sure how to tell you this but–"

"Just spit it out, Doc. The suspense is killing me."

"Mr. Jonson, it won't be the suspense that kills you. It will be Pulmortussis."

"Pull-my-what-sis?"

"Pulmortussis. Literally translates to lung death cough. The last known case of this particular disease was in Germany more than one hundred years ago. During the early 1940s it was responsible for killing thousands of German citizens. The Americans thought it was a new form of bio-weapon Hitler had created, and the Germans thought the Americans had released a weaponized version of the black plague. Unfortunately, the incubation time varied so wildly that it was deemed unreliable for use as a weapon. It was considered as effective as dusting the enemy landscape with asbestos fibers, with very similar effects and symptoms. However, it was much more aggressive. Like asbestos, it could sit dormant in your lungs for years or even decades before showing itself, but when it became active, it would attack every fiber in the lungs at the same time. The good news is that we caught it before it advanced too far and with some precautions we can keep you from spreading it..."

"And the bad news is..."

The doctor looked down at the floor before answering.

"The bad news is nothing I can do will increase your chances of survival."

Mr. Jonson looked down at the floor. After a few minutes of silence, he finally asked the question that was weighing on his mind.

"OK, Doc, how long do I have left? A few years? Months? Should I even bother going home? And don't bother sugar coating it either."

The doctor shifted on his stool for a moment before answering. "Mr. Jonson–"

"Please, call me David. I have so few friends left in this world. I would rather have a friend tell me bad news than someone in an official position." David cracked a grin before continuing, "And with all the tests and exams you have performed on me, we at least need to be on a first name basis."

The doctor chuckled and relaxed a bit, relieved that his patient still had a sense of humor to deal with his situation.

"Very well, David. Call me Steve. As for how much time you have left, I am not entirely certain. You may have as much as six to twelve months, or you could only have a few weeks. As I said before, the last recorded case of this particular disease was quite a while ago and several thousand miles away, which leads me to wonder how you came into contact with the virus in the first place. Have you ever been to Germany?"

David directed a stern glare at Martin.

"Not by choice, Steve. Not by choice."

Chapter 9
Finding the Second Piece

After my deployment and my return to the States, I started doing some research on the possible whereabouts of the missing items. Thinking back to my basic training days, I remembered a conversation I'd had with my battle buddy while we were digging our fox hole. When I asked why he joined the Army, he told me that he couldn't see himself following in his father's footprints and becoming a jeweler. He had then told me of how his father had been trying all his life to create a piece of jewelry that could make even the homeliest person look beautiful. I remembered my doubt that it could be done and my disbelief when he told me it already had been. He had gone on to explain that an English master jeweler had produced a necklace of such ability for his daughter's sixteenth birthday in order to make her irresistible to potential suitors. His daughter's name was Godgifu, or as history knows her, Godiva. The necklace had worked, and soon after, she was married to Leofric, Earl of Mercia.

During all of my research, I could find nothing claiming that Lady Godiva's father was a jeweler. The only reference I could find said that he was from a small village south of Egremont, England, and most likely a fisherman by trade. If that was true, then it was very possible that he could have been the same fisherman who rescued the floundering servant. As I pored though the history books, I learned of Lady Godiva's nude ride through her town in order to convince her husband to lower the taxes and that she is still considered a heroine. Thinking back to the genie's warning about changing the past, I dove further into the history books to see what I could dig up.

Upon further investigation, I discovered that after her death all of Lady Godiva's belongings were kept on display in her estate in Coventry, England, until early 1940 when they were transported to a safe house in Farthingloe, where the necklace was reportedly stolen during a German air strike against the city. Several hundred were killed during the bombing, including the person in charge of safeguarding the Godiva exhibit. Without thinking, I grabbed the globe, spun the rings on the South Pole to set the date for July 6. 1940, zero eight hundred hours, placed my right index finger on Farthingloe, and spoke aloud, "I want to be there."

With a bright flash and an intense wave of nausea I found myself falling into a storm tossed sea. Confusion gave way to anger as I remembered the accuracy problem with transporting into new areas. I looked down at the globe and watched as the blue ring slowly contracted down to a blue dot on my current location. According to the globe, I was only a mile or so from shore, the French shore. I placed the globe in the cargo pocket of my uniform pants, kicked off my boots, removed my uniform jacket, and started to swim southeast toward the distant shoreline.

When I reached the shore and stumbled up onto the beach, my middle school history lessons on World War II came rushing back to me with a single shouted command.

"HALT!"

About thirty yards up the beach were two German soldiers with automatic rifles. I reached for my pocket in an attempt to retrieve the globe and get away, but as I started to move, one of the soldiers fired off a warning shot into the dirt at my feet. I raised my hands and stared down my captors defiantly–

"Sir, that is not exactly–"

"Martin, this is my story not yours. If I am about to

kick the bucket, and this book is going to be my mark in this world, I don't want everyone to know that when I was faced with the possibility of death, my first reaction was completely involuntary and very embarrassing. We can just leave it out of the book."

"But, Sir, the fact that your soiled clothing kept you from being searched properly so that the globe was not confiscated is a big part of the story. Without the globe, you would have never made it out of captivity."

"Are you saying that I couldn't have figured out a way to escape from them without–"

"I am not doubting any of your abilities of that time. All I am stating is that if you are going to market this book as anything other than fiction, you need to tell your story correctly."

"Just blame their ineptitude for missing the globe during their search."

"As you wish, Sir."

As the soldiers approached me, they started shouting orders in German. When I didn't move or say anything, one of them struck me in the back with the stock of his rifle, dropping me to my knees and then shoved me down onto my stomach. After a very brief search, I was hauled back to my feet and marched to a waiting military truck where I was bound hand and foot and tossed into the back. Relief flooded through me as I realized that the globe was still in my cargo pocket even though I couldn't get to it with my hands bound behind my back.

The only thing I could discern from what little I could see out the back of the truck was that we were headed east. The only thing I could think of that was east of where I had come ashore was the German border. We rode for what seemed like hours. I couldn't imagine what they would do to me when they found out that I was an American, nor could I imagine the damage that would be done to the timeline if Hitler were to gain possession of the globe. I had to come up with a plan of escape.

When we finally reached our destination the sun had disappeared beneath the horizon, and I was battered and bruised from being bounced around. The two soldiers who had collected me on the beach removed me from the back of the truck and deposited me on the ground in front of an older German officer. The officer looked down at me and spoke something in German. Judging correctly that I didn't understand him, he spoke again, this time in French. After shaking my head no and shrugging my shoulders, he spoke once more, finally in English.

"Who do you work for and where are you from?"

Thinking quickly, I spoke in a language that I was sure this man had never heard.

"jIyajbe'"

The officer stared at me for a moment trying to figure out what I had said.

I tried another phrase on him, "nuqneH"

Confused, the officer spoke to the two soldiers and pointed at a small brick building on the other side of the yard. As the soldiers started to drag me off, I yelled out one more phrase in order to further confuse my captors, if not about my nationality, then of my sanity.

"Hab SoSlI' Quch!"

"Sir, if I may ask, what exactly were you saying? That is not a language that I am familiar with."

David looked at his butler in astonishment.

"Surely you have heard that language before. I learned it in high school. Not from any classes offered there, just during that time. All my friends called me either a dork or a

dweeb for being able to speak it. They told me there would never be a practical use for the Klingon language in my future, but it saved my life, didn't it!"

"If you say so, Sir. You still have not answered my question. What did you say?"

"First I said, 'I don't understand.' Then I asked him, 'What do you want?' Lastly, I told them all that their mothers had smooth foreheads. In Klingon, that's a huge insult."

"Your friends may have been correct."

"Excuse me?"

"Nothing, Sir."

"Let's get back to the book."

When we reached the brick building, I was tossed inside what looked like a small cleaning closet. I looked around and quickly located a mop with a metal handle leaning against the wall. The end of the handle looked pretty sharp, so I wiggled my way over to it, knocked it over, and started to rub the ropes that bound my hands against the sharp edge. After five minutes or so, I was through the ropes and my hands were free. I untied my feet, stood up and reached into my pocket, which to my horror, was completely empty. The globe was gone.

The bruise on my leg was proof that it was in my pocket when I was thrown into the truck; however, I couldn't recall feeling it when I was pulled out. Since nobody had searched me since our arrival at this small base, I could only assume that it was still in the back of the truck.

I tried the door and found that it wasn't locked. I opened it up a crack and peeked out. What I saw chilled me to the bone. The building I had been tossed into was some sort of weapons stockpile. It was filled with racks and racks of explosives, from grenades to satchel charges.

Stacked against the back wall were large drums that

were painted black with a white skull and cross bones as
well as a picture of a gas mask on the side. Part of me knew I
should try not to interfere with what happened in the past, but
the rest of me knew that I couldn't let these weapons be used
against the allied forces if it was in my power to prevent it.
I grabbed all of the satchel charges I could carry and packed
them around the black drums. I walked over to the exterior
door and tried the knob. To my astonishment, it wasn't locked
either. Peeking out, I could see the two soldiers talking to the
older officer near another building off to my right. The truck
was twenty or twenty-five yards to my left, but I was pretty
sure I could make it if I ran. Besides, once the charges started
going off they would have bigger things to worry about.

I walked back to the satchel charges and pulled the tabs,
igniting the fuses. Unsure of how long it would take for them
to explode, I ran for the door. Pausing only long enough to
find the three Germans again, I threw the door open and made
a mad dash for the truck. The charges blew just as the first
soldier brought up his rifle, and the explosion spoiled his aim.
His bullet passed just by my right ear and struck the back
of the truck. As I dove into the bed of the truck, a second
explosion several times bigger than the first erupted from the
stockpile spreading debris and a thick wall of smoke all over
the base. I frantically searched for the globe as I started to
choke on the fumes. When I found it, I placed my finger in
the middle of England and screamed the proper words just as
a huge fireball consumed the entire base.

With my breath held and my eyes tightly shut I braced
for another swim, but to my amazement, my feet were set on
solid ground. Looking at the globe, I watched as the blue ring
shrank down to a blue dot in the middle of England, almost
exactly where I had chosen.

"I'm impressed, Genie. I half expected to wind up in the
middle of a lake or maybe downtown London."

"I do not always miss that badly. I told you that I could only guarantee to get you within thirty miles. Actual distance from target varies."

Squinting in the harsh morning sunshine, I felt that something wasn't quite right. Curiosity got the better of me and I turned the globe over to check the date. Nothing had been changed accidentally during transport. Then it dawned on me. When I had started the jump, I hadn't reset the time on the bottom of the globe, so I had once again jumped to eight in the morning on July 6th. A brief mental image of a madman driving a beat up pick-up with a rodent hanging on the steering wheel made me chuckle. Checking the map again, I turned south and started my journey to Farthingloe. In the distance I could just make out the storm clouds over the English Channel.

As I drew near my destination, I started to notice smoke coming from just over the horizon. Remembering what was going on during this time period in England, I prepared myself for what might be a gruesome sight. As I crested the last hill, I saw what was left of the town of Farthingloe. The image shook me to the core, and I had to resist the urge to use the globe to go back and prevent the war from ever starting. I made my way into the city and looked around at all the damage done by the German bombers.

One of the buildings that was destroyed was a shoe shop. With my boots still located at the bottom of the English Channel, I looked around and selected a pair from the rubble that fit fairly well and put them on. Walking around the decimated city, I began to wonder if I would be able to find the supposed safe house where all of Lady Godiva's stuff had been moved to. I remembered from my research that it had been a large building within sight of a clock tower and that it had been largely untouched by the bombings.

I walked into a large square in the middle of the town

where people were milling about trying to find loved ones, or just staring off into space. Considering what I had been through, or would go through later that day depending on your point of view, I looked just as ragged as the rest of the populace. A very plain-looking lady in her early fifties came up to me and placed a blanket around my shoulders and asked me where I was from. I told her I had been spending some time with relatives just outside of town when the bombers came, and I was the only survivor out of the whole group of us.

When she heard my accent, she knew right away that I wasn't English and she just had to ask why I had come to England during the war.

"Well, ma'am, I am a bit of a history nut and I have been doing research on Lady Godiva. My uncle told me that they had her stuff on display up in Coventry. Unfortunately, by the time I got up there all of her stuff had been taken to a safe house in an undisclosed city. I just wish I could have seen it before it was hauled off."

"Young man, you are in luck. It just so happens that I am the curator of the Lady Godiva museum. If you would like, I could take you to see the collection right now."

"That would be wonderful! How could I repay you?"

She looked at me with a warm smile.

"You don't have to, love. Just having someone willing to see the collection is payment enough."

We walked together for a couple blocks until we came upon a large building. She unlocked the front door and let me in. There, laid out in rows and rows of display cases, were all of the belongings of Lady Godiva, along with artistic renditions of her famed ride through Coventry. As I walked down the row of jewelry, I began to wonder if I would be able to pick out the right necklace. I turned to my guide and asked her if she knew of the necklace given to Lady Godiva by her father on her sixteenth birthday.

"My, you are quite the history buff, aren't you. Not many people know of that necklace and even fewer know of its significance. Do you know of the power it holds?"

"I have heard rumors, ma'am, but I am not sure I believe them. That was one of the things I was hoping to find out during my trip."

"All the rumors are true, and just so you don't have to take my word for it, follow me."

She went to the back of the room to a small safe that was bolted to the floor. After entering the combination, she pulled out a small box. Within the box was a delicate golden necklace with a small charm that looked like a blooming rose growing from a lovers knot. Handing me the necklace, she turned her back to me and pulled her hair up. I removed the necklace from the box and placed it around her neck. Instantly her hair became long and turned a shimmering blonde, the lines on her face disappeared, and she shed forty pounds and at least twenty-five years. Stepping back, I had to catch my breath as she spun to show off her beauty.

"What do you think?"

I stuttered a few times before I could answer coherently.

"Wha... Whoa... Wow! It really works! You, my Lady, have become the most beautiful woman I have ever seen."

Just then the air raid sirens began to blare, warning of an imminent strike. Panic gripped the curator and she started running for the door. I yelled for her to stop, knowing that this building was one of the few structures that survived the war. Before I could stop her, she had run out into the street and was well on her way to a known bomb shelter in the area. She never made it. A German plane flew overhead and released its deadly cargo of bombs, wiping out a building and spraying debris all over the road. The curator was buried in the rubble and was killed almost instantly. I ran down the street to see if there was any hope of saving her, but I knew at once it was too late. I gently removed the necklace from her neck and watched as her broken body reverted back to its previous homeliness.

I walked back to the building where the rest of the collection was stored and looked around. A deep feeling of sadness filled my heart as I realized what obtaining my goal had cost. Pulling the globe out of my pocket, I placed my right index finger on the red dot indicating my starting point and said aloud, "I want to go back."

Chapter 10
Time Patching

Several weeks after I retrieved the necklace, I was faced with a very serious question: whether or not to reenlist in the Army. On one hand, I had seen the horrors of war, both modern and 1940s variations, and didn't really want to do it again. On the other hand, I didn't have anywhere else to go. As I sat down with the retention NCO, a small, rotund man with an artificial leg and a severe lack of hair, he asked me where I saw myself in twenty to thirty years.

"Honestly, Sergeant, if you had asked me that before my deployment I would have said that I would still be in uniform serving my country. But now, I am not so sure. Knowing what you know now, what would you do?"

The NCO sat for a moment and unconsciously rubbed his prosthetic limb.

"Knowing what I know now... Let's see... I would probably have chosen not to reenlist just before I went on the mission that took my leg. Furthermore, if I had all the info available to me now, I would take out my savings and play the stock market. That way I could invest in something that I knew would grow. But since I had nowhere to go, no foreknowledge to make money with, and no civilian job to fall back on, I chose to reenlist. But this is not about my life choices, this is about yours."

I thought about my options for a moment. Staying in the service would give me a steady paycheck with which I could finance the search for the rest of the pieces. However, it would make my life more complicated if I ever had to explain injuries I receive during any of my missions. If I chose to get out, I would be able to devote all my time to my quest. The problem was in funding my research and expeditions. Travel wouldn't be a problem, the globe would take care of that. The problem would be buying supplies, both in the present and the past. It was at that moment that the last comment the recruiter made finally clicked. *Go into the past with knowledge of stocks and play the market.*

I stood up from the table, shook the recruiter's hand, and thanked him for his time. "Thank you, Sergeant, but I believe I will be happy to hang up my uniform and leave it here."

"If you ever change your mind, Specialist, feel free to give me a call."

I thanked him again and left his office. I had less than a week until my obligation to the Army was up, and I wanted to use the resources available to plan the next phase of my search.

One week later I was ready. I turned in all my gear to the supply sergeant, said my goodbyes to all the guys in my unit, and at eleven o'clock I made my way off post. Everything that I owned, which wasn't much, was packed neatly into a blue backpack. I had one change of civilian clothes, my toothbrush, several pages of stock market notes from 1990 to the present, the necklace I had retrieved, and the globe.

I walked into the city park which was just outside the main gate of the base. It seemed fairly quiet in the park that afternoon, with only one other person around–a young man in ripped up blue jeans, blue T-shirt, a pair of cheap sunglasses, and a faded black ball cap. He was smoking a thin cigar with a plastic tip and leaning up against a tree next to the walking path that wound its way through the park, about twenty or so feet from the nearest bench. As I sat on the bench to try and decide on the best place to start my investments, the young man tossed his cigar onto the path, reached behind his back and started toward me. For a brief second I thought I was going to be mugged, or worse, murdered. I started to stand up to vacate the area when I was hit with an intense wave of vertigo. The sensation only lasted for a second or two, but when I recovered, the young man was gone along with the cigar he had discarded on the path. Confused, I turned around, looking everywhere for my would-be mugger, but he was nowhere to be seen.

I looked down at my backpack, and to my astonishment, there was a note sticking out of the top of it. What really got me interested was that the note was addressed to me and was in my own handwriting.

David,

If you are reading this then I/you/we were successful in changing the timeline. However, as you can imagine, steps must be taken to ensure that time does not revert back to the way it was. Check your watch NOW! Take the globe and set the time to twenty-six minutes ago, using your current location as your destination in the past. With the inaccuracy problem the globe has you will arrive on the other side of the park just outside the east gate, a little over a half mile away. When you arrive, there will be a patrol car parked in an alley approximately thirty or so feet to your northeast in between two dumpsters. The officer will be sitting in the car and should just be finishing up his lunch. Walk over to his car and tell him that you have seen what you believe to be a large pistol in the waistband of a man wearing ripped up blue jeans, blue T-shirt, a pair of cheap sunglasses, and a faded black ball cap. If I/you have timed this letter correctly, the suspect will walk right by the front of the officer's car just as you finish describing him. At that point, you need to yell, "There he is!" The officer will get out of his car and walk toward Mr. Ball Cap. When the officer puts his hand on his hip, dive immediately to your left behind the large green dumpster. After a brief altercation, the officer will be forced to run down Mr. Ball Cap on foot. As soon as they disappear around the building, run as fast as you can to the bench you are sitting on now. You will see yourself start to stand up, suffer from what appears to be an intense wave of vertigo, and fall back down, dropping the backpack you found

this letter in. While he/you are down, place this letter on the top
of the backpack and immediately use the globe to return to your
own time, completing the circle. Believe me, failure to follow
these instructions will result in a gunshot wound to the right
leg, a two-year hunt to find the globe, and complete loss of the
necklace.

    Good luck!

    David Jonson

    P.S. Don't worry about your previous self seeing you.
The vertigo caused by the change in the timeline will keep him
down long enough to place the note. Be aware that the timeline
will not change instantly. The change will propagate out from
the point of change at the speed of the change, dissipating with
distance like ripples in a pond when a rock is thrown in, until
everything is changed or time catches up with the present time.
So you will have about six minutes after Mr. Ball Cap runs
away to place the note before the wave hits your previous self.
For example: you did not change what you were going to do
until you perceived Mr. Ball Cap as a threat. When you stood
up to leave and suffered vertigo, that was the time wave passing
over you. Time changes happen more often than you might
think. If it is a minor change to your recent past it is usually
experienced as dejá-vu or false memories. Major changes or
changes to the distant past will have larger impacts, such as
vertigo or just a feeling that things are not as they are supposed
to be. Just think of every time you thought you saw someone
you haven't seen in several years in your peripheral vision, only
to turn back and see someone completely different. Or you walk
into a room and cannot remember why you went in there. This
is possibly a "time wave" passing over you.

    Additional instructions: Due to the number of times this
letter has made, or will make the loop, if it is in poor condition,
rewrite it EXACTLY as it is."

    I folded up the note and placed it in my pocket, set the
destination time on the bottom of the globe, and activated
the transport. After a brief flash, I found myself right where

the note had said. I ran over to the cop car and knocked on the window. Startled, the officer rolled down his window and asked me where the fire was. I quickly described Mr. Ball Cap, and true to the letter, the suspect rounded the corner just as I finished my statement. I pointed at him and screamed, "THERE HE IS!" The letter's instructions were pretty clear on what my next action should be; however, it never occurred to me what it meant by a "brief altercation." As soon as the words left my lips, the young man drew his firearm and let off three or four rounds in our direction. For a brief second I was paralyzed with fear, not of the gunman, but the fact that the note was wrong about the order of events. The cop was supposed to get out of the car before anything happened. I tried to think if I had done something wrong, but I was shaken out of my reverie by the snap of a bullet passing uncomfortably close to my left ear. Adrenalin surged through my veins and forced me into action. I threw myself to my right behind a dumpster for cover, only to realize that I had mistakenly gotten behind the red one instead of the green one, as the instructions dictated. Panic gripped me, for there had to be a reason that the instructions had specified the green dumpster. Looking around I discovered why. Stacked along the wall just behind me were a number of propane tanks. If a stray bullet caught one of those I would be hard pressed to get to my earlier self in time. Then again, if I never made it to myself, I wouldn't receive the note, and I wouldn't have come back in the first place. A dull ache started to form just behind my right eye. I swore to myself never to get involved in another time loop again.

When the officer finally got out of his car and returned fire, I crawled as fast as I could behind his car to the green dumpster. Just as I made it to safety, a stray round impacted one of the tanks causing it to explosively decompress, showering the back of the red dumpster with shrapnel and propane. I thought about modifying the note to warn my past self about the propane tanks but decided against it. Had I known about the shootout I might have hesitated and caused a bigger problem. At that moment, the officer and Mr. Ball Cap decided to make their exit. I checked my watch. Eight minutes to go before catching up to my departure time, so I had about six minutes to deliver the note. I sprinted to the east gate of the park, and in the distance I could see a figure just entering the west gate. I ran as hard as I could toward the bench where my previous self would sit. As I ran, I watched the other me approach the bench. I was only fifteen or so feet away when I noticed a ghostly image of Mr. Ball Cap throw down his cigar and leave his spot against the tree. My earlier self saw him and started to rise. I pulled out the note and thrust it into the top the backpack where I found it. As soon as the note touched the backpack everything around me shimmered like a desert mirage and Mr. Ball Cap faded away. I grabbed the globe, touched my starting point, said the magic phrase, and with a flash I was back where I started. This particular transport was a little more disorienting than the few others I had experienced. I didn't actually move. My previous self disappeared, and several leaves jumped a few feet because of the slight breeze that had been blowing.

The world shifting around me made my head spin and I lost my balance. I sat down on the bench and stared at the globe. If anyone could give me some answers as to what just happened it would be the genie.

"All right, Genie. What in the world just happened? I somewhat understand the whole time patch idea with the note, however, the note was wrong. What did I do contrary to the instructions provided to me?"

The globe vibrated slightly with the voice of the genie.

"You did what you were meant to do. If you had been given every detail you would have been too caught up in reproducing everything exactly as the letter had said. Had the note been perfectly accurate in its description of the events to unfold, you would not have panicked and had that rush of adrenalin. You did not even notice that when you threw yourself at the red dumpster, you actually jumped over the hood of the police car. Had you gone for the green dumpster directly, you would more than likely have taken a round in the shoulder from the officer when he returned fire through his window. What was written was meant to be written and you were meant to follow it as you did."

I rubbed my temple as the dull ache behind my right eye returned. "Genie, is this going to be a common occurrence? Am I going to have to keep going back to save myself and risk creating multiple paradoxes? I have seen movies where people cheat death with the foreknowledge of how they die, and none of those people lasted too long."

The genie was silent for a moment before answering. "Only time will tell."

Frustrated, I stuffed the globe back into the backpack and retrieved the stock sheets. I had to find a good starting point for my investments. I remembered the old adage "It takes money to make money," and I knew where I could get some quick cash in the past. After an hour or two, I had my plans drawn up. Reluctantly, I pulled out the globe and set my desired time. With one last look around to make sure nobody was watching, I set my destination for just outside my hometown and was once again whisked into the past.

Chapter 11
Changing The Past

I reappeared on May 23, 1991, at six fifteen in the evening. I looked around trying to get my bearings and I recognized the tower of the local airport in the distance. With a roar, a small Cessna zoomed over my head, missing me by mere inches. The pilot must have flared his aircraft in order to avoid making a mess of me all over the tarmac. Instead of climbing back up to fly around and try his landing again, the pilot stalled the little airplane and set it back down close to the end of the runway. Without enough room to do a roll out he carried on past the end of the runway and out into the grass. The pilot tried to make a hard right turn to stop the aircraft but still managed to clip some trees with his left wingtip, severely damaging the wing.

I stuck around only long enough to see the pilot climb out of the crippled craft before I made my escape. I made a mental note to look up aviation accident investigations for the Flying Dollar Airport when I got back to my own time, just to see how my sudden appearance was explained.

"Did you ever look up that information, Sir?"

"Yeah. The NTSB just wrote it off as pilot error–something about landing downhill and downwind. I'm just grateful that he saw me in time to miss me. It would have been difficult to come back and save myself from that situation. The thought of yet another paradox still makes my head hurt, right there." David rubbed his right temple.

"I can see where they can be a little daunting."

"Daunting is not the word for it, Martin."

May 23, 1991, was a day that I remembered very well from my youth. It was the day that we went on vacation to visit relatives down south only to return to a house that had been ransacked and burned to the ground. The police report stated that the blaze was set around midnight the night we left. What wasn't stolen was destroyed in the fire. Some of the more expensive stuff was eventually found at a local pawn shop, but most of the stuff the thieves took was never recovered.

I made it within sight of my parents house just in time to see the entire family, including a younger me, drive off in our old mint green station wagon. Seeing the house I grew up in brought back a flood of memories. It was a single story house with three bedrooms and a single bathroom that we all had to share. The brown paint on the outside of the house was peeling in several places around the large picture window that looked out of the living room. The only door to the house was underneath a small covered carport with two small concrete steps leading up to it.

I checked my watch; it was just after eight, and the moon was just barely peeking out from behind the cloud cover. The key for the door was exactly where I remembered, underneath a small piece of broken concrete on the bottom step. I unlocked the door and made my way into the house. As I stepped into the house, I was greeted with the smell of vanilla from one of my mother's favorite candles that was still burning on the coffee table in the middle of the living room. Moving swiftly and silently, I went into my bedroom, took one of my pillow cases, and moved through the house gathering everything of value that I could fit into it. In my parent's bedroom, behind the family portrait, was the wall safe that my father had insisted on installing when we moved in. My mother could never remember the combination, so in her infinite wisdom, she wrote the numbers on the back of the portrait. I was a little surprised to find that the combination was my birth date, and it caused me to pause for a second and rethink what I doing. I shook my head and remembered that what wasn't stolen was lost in the fire, so I continued on with my mission. Inside the safe I hit the jackpot. There were two five thousand dollar bearer bonds. No wonder my father had been so devastated when he found out that the safe had survived the fire, but was found empty. The dates on the bonds stated that they would not mature for another ten years or so, but that wouldn't be a problem, I could always go forward and cash them out.

As I continued my search of the house I began to wonder where the real criminals were that had broken into our house. I checked my watch. Eleven forty-five. The person or persons responsible for changing my life should have been here by now. I walked into the living room and peeked out the window through the curtains at the empty lawn. The furnace decided to come on at that moment with a loud pop. The sound made me jump back from the window and I tripped over the coffee table, turning it over and spilling everything that was on it, including the vanilla candle, onto the thick shag carpeting. The candle bounced once and rolled across the floor leaving a trail of fire in its wake. It came to a stop against the side of the couch and promptly set it ablaze as well.

I stood there in bewilderment, dumbstruck with the realization that there had never been any thieves, only me. The guilt mounted as the flames crawled up the wall and engulfed the entire room. I decided it was a good time to make my exit and ran out the door with my bag of loot. When I was safely away, I had the thought that if I hadn't come back and destroyed my house, my life would have turned out a bit differently, and I might not have joined the military. If I hadn't joined and deployed, I wouldn't have found the globe,

which means I couldn't have come back and robbed myself...
So how exactly did I come back and rob... My head started to
throb as I tried to work my way through the paradox. I pulled
out the globe and presented my question to the genie.

"Genie, how is it possible that I robbed myself in order
to profit from a robbery that I remembered, when I was
in fact the only robber the entire time? If I hadn't robbed
myself, I wouldn't have remembered it and I wouldn't have
come back to profit from it."

Once again the globe pulsed with its answer, and I could
swear that it was laughing at me although its voice gave no
hint of amusement.

"Originally, the house just burnt down because of the
candle on the coffee table. When you came back to rob the
house, your memories changed as you carried out your plan."

"So what happened to the whole nausea-inducing, time
wave?"

"The timeline did not change until you opened the safe.
It was not until then that the police suspected anything other
than a tragic accident. Since it did not change your actions,
the only effect it had on you made you pause and rethink
what you were doing. Had it been a larger change, the effects
would have been greater."

"Like when I was incapacitated in the park?"

"Exactly."

I began to wonder just how many paradoxes I was going
to create in my life time. I took out the bonds and checked
the date, June 11, 2001. I laughed to myself as I realized I
was going to create yet another one.

*"Martin, you really want to tell everyone about the
chicken plant don't you."*

*"We have to, Sir. It is yet another example of how
profoundly the globe effected your life, before and after you*

found it. Besides, you told me when we started this that I could find a way to work it in later."

"I said you would *find a way to work it in. Not that you* could *or even* should. *But, I am too tired to fight about it so just make it quick."*

"As you wish."

"Don't give me that! If it were truly as I wished, then you wouldn't do it at all. And further more—" David collapsed back onto the couch where he was sitting in a coughing fit. Martin was at his side instantly.

"Sir, are you alright? We can stop for the day if you need to rest."

David recovered enough to push Martin back.

"No, I am not alright. You know as well as I do that I am not long for this world, so if it is alright with you, I would like to finish these memoirs. Even if it means letting you explain to the world how I wound up in a chicken suit, chasing reflections, and causing the largest industrial disaster in poultry processing history."

"Thank you, Sir."

"Just make sure you explain it correctly."

The Gomez Brand Chicken Processing Plant had been in operation since before the Second World War. The only part of the plant that was ever updated was the paint on the exterior of the building. When I started working there, shortly after the Camaro incident, the outside of the plant was painted a bright green which clashed horribly with the neon yellow smiling chicken face logo that was displayed proudly above the main entrance. The plant itself was huge, with almost four hundred thousand square feet of interior floor space, filled wall to wall with everything necessary to turn a live chicken into a frozen package of breasts, thighs, wings, and drumsticks. On the eastern end of the plant was the receiving department and chicken storage, where billions and billions of chickens saw their last bit of sunlight before being processed. On the western end was the shipping department, where those same chickens were loaded into tractor trailer freezer trucks and sent on to the grocery stores of America.

The chickens passed from the receiving department, cage and all, on conveyor belts into the cleaning room, where they were blasted with superheated steam which deprived them of their feathers as well as their lives. It also had the added benefit of cleaning the cages out. From there they were removed from the cages and processed by–

"Martin, when I said explain it correctly I didn't mean the gruesome processing details. I was talking about the accident."

"But Sir, the reader needs to know why you took the position in the suit to begin with. They may not understand your decision to give up fifteen dollars an hour riding a forklift in an air-conditioned plant for a ten-dollar-an-hour position in a chicken suit outside the plant."

"It was an advertising gig, and anyone who has been in a chicken plant would know that the smell alone would be enough to drive someone to seek a different method of earning convertible debentures. Of course, it wasn't the smell that drove me out. It was the screams of the chickens when the steam hit them, but you don't need to put that into the book. Just skip to what I was doing there."

Martin raised an eyebrow inquisitively, "Which time, Sir?"

"The second time, Martin."

After pawning off the rest of the items I "saved" from the fire, I bought a decent suit and a soft-sided, black leather briefcase to hold the bonds, the necklace, the globe and the stock sheets. I threw away all of my other clothes because I wanted to look professional when I visited the bank. I checked to make sure I had everything I needed and once again used the globe to jump in time.

The chicken plant was located about fifteen miles from the bank where the bonds were drawn. In an attempt to miss the plant entirely and to avoid the mayhem that I knew was going to ensue, or had ensued, depending on how you look at it, I selected the plant as my destination hoping that the inherent inaccuracy of the globe would put me somewhere else entirely. I appeared in a small cleaning closet that reminded me of the one I was held captive in sixty-one years ago. Chuckling to myself, I pulled out the globe to ask where we were. The globe hummed and pulsed slightly, but before it could answer the smell of burnt feathers and chicken manure overwhelmed me, and I thought I was going to be sick. The genie almost sounded pleased as he verbalized what my nose had already confirmed.

"Master, I believe we have landed within fifteen feet of your desired target location."

"Gee, thanks."

Cautiously, I eased the door open. I found myself in the management office area located on the second floor of the northwestern corner of the plant. It consisted of a large open room with four cubicles in the center. Behind a door on the east end of the room was a stairwell that led down to the production line and on the west end of the room was short hallway that led back to a small waiting area with three doors, one on each wall. The door on the north wall of the waiting area led to a small locker room, the one on the west wall led to the plant supervisor's office, and the southern door led to the cleaning closet I was currently occupying. The office area was far enough away from the line that you couldn't hear the death rattles of the poultry, but obviously not far enough to avoid the smell. I had set my entry time for seven in the morning to give myself plenty of time to make it to the bank no matter how far away I appeared. That worked to my advantage. At ten minutes to seven everybody in the office would walk down to the line and meet with the supervisors to get the numbers from the night shift, and they didn't return until seven-fifteen. The only person I would have to watch out for was my younger self, who, if I remembered correctly, should have already changed into that hideous chicken costume and made his way out to the front of the plant.

When I was only five or so feet from the door to the stairway, the handle began to turn and I could hear two distinct voices behind the door. The first voice sounded familiar but I couldn't place it. However, the other made my hair stand on end. It was my own voice, only younger. Memories of this day flooded my mind, and I could remember returning to the office area to retrieve the head to my costume while talking to someone claiming to be an investigative reporter. I had opened the door and seen what appeared to be an older version of myself sprinting for the back office.

The door opened and for a brief second I made eye contact with myself and the reporter before turning on my heel and dashing back down the short hallway toward the supervisor's office. Behind me I could hear the rustle of feathers as my younger self gave chase. There was one other exit from the second floor; the only problem was it had a sensor on it that would set off an alarm in the plant, specifically, the fire alarm. I ran into the supervisor's office and pulled the door shut behind me. There wasn't a lock on the handle, so I kicked the small plastic door wedge underneath it to jam it shut. I ran over to the fire door and tried to run through it. It didn't move. I set down my briefcase and rubbed my shoulder. The pounding on the office door became more intense, and the wedge began to give under the assault. I took a running start, jumped into the air, and kicked the fire door as hard as I could. The door flew open, and I tumbled head over heels down the fire escape and into the back parking lot. I laid on the ground for a moment, amazed that I hadn't broken anything during my less-than-graceful decent. I was shaken from my musings by the Klaxon alarms starting up all over the plant signaling for evacuation, and with a start I realized that my briefcase was still in the supervisor's office.

The evacuation couldn't exactly be described as orderly. During the annual fire drills, everyone would move quickly and quietly to their designated area. Whenever we had a drill, I always heard someone ask the question, "What could possibly burn in a steel and concrete building?" And one day our safety department answered that question with one of their own. "What do you think fuels our boilers for the steam?" After that day, people began to wonder if they would be able to get far enough away in the event of a fire. They had a legitimate reason to worry, too. The boilers ran off of natural gas. But instead of a gas line from the local supplier, the plant had two giant three-hundred-thousand-gallon tanks that were filled once or twice a month. The safety department explained what would happen if one of those tanks caught fire and exploded and showed us pictures of similar plants that had suffered from just such a disaster.

This was not a drill, and thanks to the safety departments in depth description, people were screaming and running over each other trying to get out of the plant. Three hundred panicked production workers came pouring out into the parking lot, but didn't stop there. Most of them jumped into their cars and left the area just as fast as their cars could take them. I started running back up the fire escape in hopes that

I could somehow get my briefcase back before someone, namely my younger self, got hold of it and changed the timeline. Halfway up the stairs I heard my own voice yelling at me from above. I looked up just in time to see my younger self slam the fire door, which to my dismay didn't have a handle on the outside. I quickly made my way back down the stairs and around the front of the plant and entered through the shipping department. I finally made it through the mob of evacuees just as my younger self was coming out of the office stairwell on the other side of the warehouse. He was carrying my briefcase and looking a bit confused. I yelled for him to stop where he was, but instead he took off running. About five feet from me was an abandoned forklift of the type that needed a password in order to start instead of a key. Thankfully I remembered my code. I jumped onto the lift, punched in my code, threw it into gear and took off after my feathered former self. When he saw me coming he tried to get away by running deeper into the plant, hoping to lose me around some of the corners. What he didn't know was that I knew exactly where he was going and what he was planning, but for some strange reason I was drawing a blank on how it all turned out. I knew he would be hiding behind the roll up door frame in the boiler room. I floored the throttle on the fork lift and just as I passed through the doorway, I dove off, catching him with a perfect tackle, knocking the case out of his hand and the wind out of his lungs. The forklift, with the pedal somehow stuck down, carried on into the boiler room until it struck the side of the boiler, piercing the natural gas line that fed the combustion chamber.

There was a safety shutoff valve installed on the gas line in case of a rupture, but unfortunately, that was exactly where the forks had struck the line. It didn't explode like you would see in the movies, and at first my younger self and I thought there wasn't any damage after all. That is until the strong smell of sulfur reached our noses. I grabbed the briefcase with one hand and a handful of feathered costume with the other, hauled him to his feet and half pulled, half dragged him out the nearest exit. When we were outside the plant, my memories started to clear up a bit and though I didn't remember exactly what had happened to the plant, I did remember being propped up against a huge tree and woken up with smelling salts. My younger self was beginning to become more and more combative as I forced him to the biggest tree on the lot. I couldn't remember how I had been rendered unconscious. As we passed the big tree, he finally pulled free of my grasp and demanded some answers. I stared him in the eye for a few seconds and when I had his full, undivided attention, I hit him as hard as I could with a right cross. He went down like a bag of wet sand. I propped him up against the side of the tree facing away from the plant and quickly made my escape. Just as I made it over the perimeter fence the gas in the plant found an ignition source. Half of the plant disappeared in a giant fireball and the other half fell over from the concussion. Since the alarm had gone off several minutes earlier there were no casualties in the explosion. Well, no human casualties. People would be finding feathers all over the area for the next three weeks.

"Sir, if I may ask, how did you get blamed for the destruction of the plant?"

David looked at Martin, wondering if he was even paying attention to what he was typing.

"They recovered the computer from the forklift. Apparently, those forklifts had a little black box that recorded hours driven, driving conditions, and who was driving. Since I used my old code to start the forklift and the lift was the cause of the accident, it was pretty clear to the investigators who was at fault. I tried to tell them that someone who looked

*just like me used my codes and stole the lift, but they just
laughed at me and told me that I was responsible for my
codes. My codes, my fault. I was taken before the local judge
and sentenced to community service. On the wall behind the
judge was the flier for the Army. I asked the judge if there
was a way I could serve out my sentence in the service of my
country, and he said that it wasn't a bad idea."*

Martin looked at David in astonishment.

*"Sir, do you mean to say that your choice to join the
military was not purely on a volunteer basis?"*

*David chuckled, "If by volunteer you mean that I went to
the recruiter's office and signed up all by myself, then yes, it
was voluntary. But it wasn't my first choice."*

Martin shook his head and turned back to the computer.

Several hours and fifteen miles later, I arrived at the First
Bank of Buck Hill Falls. Walking down the streets of my
home town made me kind of nervous. I wasn't sure if anyone
would recognize me or what I would do if they did. To be
honest, I wouldn't have risked coming here to cash the bonds
if I hadn't had to; unfortunately, the bonds were of the type
that could only be cashed out at the bank that issued them.
Thankfully, luck was on my side for once, and I was able to
get to the bank and cash out my bonds without incident.

I left the bank, walked down a nearby alley and pulled
out the globe. I was about to make the jump back to when I
wanted to start my investments when I had a sudden thought.
I pulled out some of the cash that I had received for the bonds
and checked the dates. Every bill I checked was brand new. I
had ten thousand dollars in cash, and it was all useless to me
in the past. I needed to find something I could purchase and
take back with me that I could sell to buy stocks. Granted,
I could have just bought stocks in 2001, but I wanted to go
back to 1996 to get well established in the market before the

dot-com boom.

   As I left the alley in search of a solution to my dilemma, I noticed a sign for the local jewelry store and just like that I had my answer. Gold. The local jewelers sold gold ingots, bars, and bullion at market value and I was pretty sure that gold would be accepted anywhere–or any*when*–that I chose to go. An hour and a half later I had bought thirty-eight, one-ounce bars of gold and had just enough money left to buy some dinner at the local burger joint and rent a room at the Buck Hills Inn.

Chapter 12
Becoming Wealthy

The next morning, after counting the gold bars for the umpteenth time, I pulled out the globe and spun the date rings on the bottom until it showed noon on April 10, 1996. I sat for a moment and contemplated my destination. I certainly didn't want to stay around here, too many people had known me. I decided that if I was going to get heavy into the stock-market, then I might as well go to New York and hire a broker right there on Wall Street. Of course, I would have to find someone who either didn't know the rules, or preferably, didn't mind breaking them from time to time, because what I had in mind could be considered beyond illegal. On the other hand, the authorities would have a hard time proving anything if they did try to prosecute me.

I selected Central Park as my destination and hoped that I would appear in a vacant area. With a flash and yet another wave of nausea, I was standing, not in Central Park, but in an alley way somewhere downtown. To make matters worse, the alley was occupied by four rather questionable individuals, all of whom were wearing the same colored hats and ominous-looking bulges near their hips underneath their hooded sweatshirts. The largest of the group stood up and started walking toward me.

"Hey, Homes, I don't know what cha think you doin' in our alley, but we don't take kindly to trespassers, so, it's gonna cost ya."

I dropped the globe into the briefcase and started to back toward the road, not sure of how to respond to him. The other three goons rose to their feet and fell in behind the first as he passed them. I glanced over my shoulder to gauge the distance to the main road. It looked like it was a little over a hundred yards, which was an easy enough distance for me to cover, unless they decided to use the firearms I suspected they had under their shirts.

The big guy spoke up again, "I don't think you heard me, Homes. I said yous gonna pay. I think we'll start with that fancy looking briefcase as the first installment."

I found my voice and answered, "And if I refuse?"

It was a bold question, too bad it sounded as if a field mouse had asked it. This earned a chuckle from the four, and I gained another few feet toward the road.

"If'n yous refuse to pay, we's gonna collect."

The big guy lifted his shirt and showed me the butt of a large automatic tucked into his pants. When I saw the pistol, I felt a familiar wave of nausea pass over me, and the image of the Camaro tumbling down the road flashed before my eyes. I thought to myself that if I got out of this alive, I would go back and create some kind of distraction in order to make my escape easier. After a few seconds passed that were devoid any kind of distraction, I began to get worried. Only three reasons came to mind for why I didn't come back and create a distraction. The first was that I didn't actually need one. While that idea brought a small amount of comfort, I didn't think it was very likely. The second was a little more worrisome, I could lose the globe here and now and not be able to come back, or go home for that matter. The last thought caused the most concern and though I tried to put it out of my mind, I couldn't help but think that this could be the end.

Fear does funny things to people. As I was considering the final possibility, the lead thug advanced on me and pulled out his pistol with malice in his eyes. As the large black instrument of death cleared his waistband, I swung my briefcase as hard as I could, striking him in the side of the head. The combined weight of the gold bars and the globe made a surprisingly efficient bludgeon. With a dull thud, all traces of hostile intentions left the big guy's face and he toppled over. For a moment, the three remaining gang members and I just stood there looking at the pile their leader had become. I tried to sneak away, and only managed to make it a few feet before I tripped over a discarded pallet and landed flat on my back. The noise of my fall shook my remaining attackers out of their shocked state, and they started after me. I scrambled to my feet and made use of some of the training the military had given me. Fourteen minutes later, I was a little over two miles away and still going. When I finally stopped, I found that I had run all the way to Wall Street. I laughed to myself thinking that the reason I hadn't gone back to interfere was because I didn't need it. I opened up the briefcase to check that I had everything, and the world seemed to come to a halt. The papers were there, and the box with the gold bars was still there, but in the bottom of pocket where I dropped the globe there was only a large hole. The globe was missing.

I made my way back to the alley hoping to find it where I had fallen. Thankfully, the four punks were nowhere to be found. However, neither was the globe. I spent the next few hours searching the alleyway for it but to no avail. Just after four o'clock, I decided that hanging around in an alley where I was almost mugged with a briefcase full of gold was not the best idea I ever had. I made my way back to the jewelry store I had passed earlier on Wall Street just as the owner was starting to close up shop. I knocked on the door and he waved me in.

The shop was small, just barely big enough to hold the two display cases and a few shoppers. One of the cases held nothing but gold–necklaces, rings, even bracelets, of all shapes and sizes. The other case held all of the precious and semiprecious stones, from Agate to Zircon. Behind the case with all the gold was the store owner. He was a small man with brown hair, piercing blue eyes, and a mouth that looked as though it liked to laugh. Hanging from a chain around his neck was a pair of jeweler's glasses, complete with the monocle over the right lens. Pinned to the left breast pocket of his tailored suit was a small nameplate indicating that his name was Sam. He smiled as I came in, and I was instantly put at ease by his charming demeanor. I walked up to the counter and returned his smile.

"Excuse me, but do you happen to know where I can find a gold broker around here?"

Sam's smile grew so large that I thought his face would split. "You, my friend, have to look no more, for you have found one. I buy and sell gold in every form imaginable, from jewelry to bullion, coins to teeth. How may I be of service?"

My first impression of Sam quickly dissolved into the grease that makes up a used car dealer.

"I am looking to sell some one-ounce gold bars. Thirty-eight of them to be exact."

Sam stroked his smooth chin, as if he had once had a beard and was now missing it. "How is it that you came to own these bars? Never mind the details. The price of gold today is three fifty an ounce, so that would bring your total to–"

"Wait a sec, I happen to know that the price of gold is just over four hundred an ounce. What kind of operation are you running here anyway?"

Sam looked startled for a moment and tried to regain his composure before continuing. "Tell you what, I will call one of my friends who works in the financial district, and I will pay you today's average price for gold."

He went over to the wall and picked up the phone. After

a short conversation with his contact, he came back over to the counter with a slightly crestfallen look on his face.

"Well, it looks like you were right about the price of gold. The high was just over four hundred. But since we agreed on the average, which was $387.87 per ounce," he pulled out a large button calculator and punched in some numbers, "that makes my final offer for the thirty-eight bars…$14,739.06."

I tried to look disappointed at the offer, but truthfully, if he hadn't set the check on the counter after he wrote it, I would have jerked his shoulder out of socket taking it.

After I left his shop, I had just enough time to stop by the bank to open up an account. With ten grand in the bank, and another four and some change in my pocket, I followed my nose to a wonderful burger joint near Battery Park.

"Sir, could you really smell the cafe all the way from Wall Street?"

"No, Martin, I couldn't. I just thought that sounded better than 'I asked a cabbie where I could find a good burger.' Besides, what do you know? You weren't there."

My first thought after stepping out of the cab was that the restaurant was smaller than the room I had in the Army. With only twelve customers, the place was nearly full to capacity. After purchasing my meal, I looked around the crowded room for a vacant seat and to my astonishment, I found a familiar face. In the back of the restaurant, sitting at a table all by herself and reading a book, was a beautiful blonde vision from my past. Of course the last time I saw her she was wearing fatigues... No, wait, that's not right, she was wearing shampoo, and if I remembered correctly, she had one heck of a right hook.

I walked up to her table and smiled. "Hi. There seems to

be a severe lack of seating here, so I was wondering if you would mind if I share this table with you."

She looked at me over her glasses with a bemused look on her face. "Why would you want to sit with me? You don't even know who I am. For all you know, I could be waiting for someone."

"Let's make a deal. I will try to guess your first name. If I get it right, then I can sit with you until your date arrives. If I fail, then I will leave and not bother you again...tonight."

The young blonde smiled, nodded, and held up three fingers. "Three guesses, hot shot, no more."

I looked deep into her ice blue eyes and made my first guess, "Janice."

She shook her head and dropped a finger. Of course, I had guessed wrong on purpose. If I had just come out and said her name she would have probably thought I was a stalker or something. I made my second guess, "Jessica."

She shook her head again and dropped a second finger and looked back down at her book.

"Susan."

She slowly set her book down on the table and returned her attention to me.

"Do I know you from somewhere?"

It was my turn to shake my head and I tried to set her at ease with a friendly smile. "No, you have never met me before tonight. Your name is written on your receipt for your meal."

She looked down at the table and there on her tray sticking out from under her basket of fries, was the receipt with her name printed clearly across the top. A smile crept its way across her lips and she pointed to the seat across from her.

"Very smooth, Sir. Very smooth. And if you would be so kind as to tell me your name?"

"David."

She plucked a fry out of her basket, dipped it in ketchup, and pointed it at me. "What do you do for a living, David?"

I took a large bite out of my burger and savored the flavor of grease, stale bread, burnt beef, old mayonnaise, and lettuce that has been sitting out all day. I set the burger down and answered her question.

"Actually, I am here to get into the stock market. I have been doing some research on some new companies that are about to go public, and I would like to get in on the action. You wouldn't happen to know where I could find a good investment broker, would you?"

She sat back and drummed her fingers on the table. After a moment or two of silence she sighed and said, "I used to. A couple of days ago I was an investment broker for one of the big companies here on Wall Street. Someone under me was getting insider information and making big money at it. When he got caught he lost everything, but since I didn't report him immediately, they fired me too."

A thought struck me. "Susan, how would you like to come work for me? With your knowledge of how things work on the market and my predictions, we could make a fortune. I don't have that much to start out with, but if you are willing to help me, I will give you twenty-five percent of whatever we make. What do you think?"

She sat and considered it for a minute and then made a counteroffer. "Fifty percent, and you tell me where you acquired your information."

"I will do the fifty percent, but with no questions asked. Just rest assured that I haven't broken any laws collecting my data." I stuck out my hand. "So, do we have a deal?"

Cautiously, she reached across the table and clasped my outstretched hand. "I guess we have a deal. When do I start? Or should I ask, where do I start?"

"That's one of the things I was hoping you could help me with. I don't know how the investment game works. All I know is what I believe the stocks will do. It's up to you to use that information to make us both filthy, stinking rich."

"Okay David, if your information is that good then we can buy an office later with the money we are going to make. Meet me here tomorrow morning at six. After breakfast we will work on making money."

I shook her hand once more and bade her farewell. It was almost seven thirty when I walked out of the restaurant and the streets were packed with hundreds of cars moving about the large city. The sidewalk was just as packed with pedestrians. It was amazing how alone you could feel in a sea of people. Nobody spoke to each other. In fact, if they hadn't been bumping into each other, I feel confident that they wouldn't even have known that there was anyone else there at all. The lack of conversation tipped me off to something else that was missing. Cell phones. In my time, everyone would have been glued to some piece of communications device or other.

"Sir, if I may ask, how do you think the mid-nineties New York compares to the New York of today?"

David thought for a moment before answering. "Well, the city itself is a lot different. For one, there are twice as many people as there were then. But, on the other hand, there is a lot less congestion on the streets. That is probably due to the Skyway-Walkways that connect every building like a giant spider web. Also, with the technological advancements in building materials, the sky scrapers of today are twice the height of the ones back then. Of course, when I was there, it was only ten years before my proper time and that was my first time to The Big Apple. But the people, the people never changed. Today they still have their multimedia devices, but a lot of them are wired directly into their brains."

"Have you ever thought about getting one of those Subcutaneous Multimedia Interfaces?"

"Martin, for as long as you have been with me, you should know the answer to that. I hate having a trained medical professional cutting on me. Why anyone would have their cell phone provider perform brain surgery on them just so they can guarantee a private conversation is way beyond my scope of comprehension. Besides, I don't want to walk around looking like I am talking to myself all the time."

Martin turned back to the computer and said under his breath, "Too late, at least with an SMI you would have an excuse."

David glared at the back of Martin's head. "I suggest you get back to work on those memoirs."

"As you wish, Sir."

The next morning I was at the restaurant bright and early. When Susan arrived, I paid for her breakfast and showed her my research material.

"Wow, how did you come up with all of this without breaking any laws? This goes way beyond insider trading. How is this even possible?" She lapsed into silence as she continued to pore through the pages.

I placed my hand in the center of the page she was reading to get her full attention.

"I can't tell you. Besides, you wouldn't believe me if I did. If you are uncomfortable with that answer, I will take my business elsewhere. Are you still with me?"

She slowly nodded her head and pulled the papers away from me. "We are going to need an office to work out of. What kind of assets do you have?"

I shrugged my shoulders, "I have ten grand in the bank and the clothes on my back. Other than the papers in front of you, that's it."

"Well, I have an office we can use for a short while, as long as it's okay with my boyfriend, James."

My face fell with the last statement, and she sensed my disappointment.

"Listen, David, you seem to be an alright guy, but I never mix business with pleasure. Had I been single, you would have blown your chances when you offered me a job anyway."

I put my hands up in surrender. "I agree wholeheartedly. My life is incredibly complicated right now. So do you think James will mind if we use what I am assuming is his office?"

"It shouldn't be a problem if we don't stay too long. If your work here is even halfway accurate, then we won't have to stay more than a week. After that we can buy an office right on Wall Street."

"I think I would prefer to build a house closer to my hometown and have my office there. Unless, of course, you or your boyfriend are not comfortable with you traveling every day and working at my house, in which case, we can buy whatever office you choose."

"Depends. Where is your hometown?"

"Buck Hill Falls, Pennsylvania. It's about a hundred miles northwest of here."

"Really? I grew up in East Stroudsburg and James has a house just fifteen minutes from town. Sure, build your house and we will work from there. Don't think that because you will live there that you are in charge." She smiled and continued, "Just remember who has control of all your money."

"Touché."

For the next few months we worked out of her boyfriend's basement office. We named our firm Jonson and

Maryweather Investments. Well, she worked. I usually made some excuse to get out of the office. Mostly, I would sneak off to the alleyway I had arrived in and search for the globe. Six months after my arrival, I had my first million in the bank and I began construction of my dream house just south of Henryville. My hopes of finding the globe had dwindled, and I came to grips with the fact that I might be stranded out of time. I decided that if I was stuck, I might as well be comfortable.

The house wasn't all that big, only four thousand square feet. It had five bedrooms, each with a private bathroom. The kitchen was one that any chef would be proud to own and just behind that was the office. The office had all the newest equipment needed to work the market and a great big overstuffed couch where I spent most of my time when I was home during business hours. But my favorite part of the house was the garage–three oversized bays, two of which had automotive lifts for my newest hobby, restoring classic cars.

For a little over a year and a half I tinkered with all sorts of old cars. I would buy one old car, fix it up, sell it, and use the money to buy another old car. I wasn't looking to make a profit–I had more than enough money–I was looking for a distraction from my growing depression. The thought that I might never be able to interact with any of my family again for fear of disrupting the timeline wore on me day in and day out.

The end of June 1998 brought with it something that had been bugging me for nearly seven years. Parked in a used car lot, in serious need of repair and restoration, was a red and black sixty-eight Camaro. Here was a chance for me to set right a great wrong that I had caused in my youth. I felt that if I could restore this car, I would quit having those visions of the other one flash through my mind every time I got into an uncomfortable situation.

For nearly three years I worked on that car while Susan worked on my portfolio. In early May of 2001, I was finally ready to take it to the DMV to apply for a tag. From there I took it to the paint shop, where I gave instructions to surprise me with the color. I told them to keep it classic, but the color was up to them. For the next two weeks I paced around the office, unable to sit still, waiting for the paint shop to call and tell me it was ready. This grated on Susan's nerves until she could take no more.

"David, I really don't mind if you are in the office, but if you don't find something to occupy yourself, I am going to have James come over and tie you to your chair. Seriously, I haven't been this annoyed with someone since the paperboy broke my garden gnome. So sit down, or else!"

The mere mention of the garden gnome brought back a flood of memories, and with the memories came the depression. I collapsed onto the couch as if someone had opened a valve and let all the air out of me.

With just the barest squeak I said, "I'm sorry."

Susan, of course, didn't know the real reason for my apology and simply turned back to her computer to make the next set of trades.

The phone rang and Susan picked it up. It was the body shop calling to say the car was ready for pick up, but even that good news couldn't bring me completely out of my slump. As a way of further apologizing to Susan, I suggested that she take the rest of the afternoon off and asked if she minded picking up the car this afternoon. Since the body shop was near her house, it didn't make sense for her to bring it back that night, so I told her to just drive it in the next morning. She agreed and started to pack up her stuff. Just before she left, the postman arrived with a package from the DMV with the new license plate for my car. I handed the package to Susan and asked her to have it installed before she left the paint shop. She took the package, and before I could ask her to do anything else, she left.

That night I went to bed early and dreamed of the first Camaro I had ever driven. I remembered seeing it for the first time and hearing the rumble of the engine. I could feel the leather of the driver's seat molding to me as I sank in behind the wheel. Just as I had the first time, I shifted the car into first gear and could feel the car respond in anticipation, as if it wanted to leap forward and devour the streets. The dream progressed and quickly turned into a nightmare as the passenger door hit the awning. I remembered trying to get out and survey the damage, and the next thing I knew, the car was being smashed to bits by a fire truck. I remembered retrieving the license plate from the wreckage and handing it to the man who had entrusted me with it. I couldn't remember the man's face too clearly, but his date looked very familiar. The fog of my dream started to pull back, and I recognized the woman standing over her date after he had passed out.

The doorbell rang, waking me from my dream. The clock by my bed read nine fifteen. I had been asleep for only a couple of hours. I quickly threw on a robe and made my way to the front door, where I was greeted by a very distraught Susan. Her boyfriend was standing beside her with a small metal object in his hands. It was a license plate. Before either of them could say anything, I took the plate away from him and read the numbers, AXE 248. I started to chuckle. Susan and James just stared at me for a moment as if I had lost my mind.

When I finally regained my composure, I asked them a simple question. "So, they chose to paint the car blue, right?" I stepped into the house and beckoned them both inside.

Susan entered the house and pulled James into the living room. As she sat down on the couch she said, "You would have loved it. Dark blue with white racing stripes. Very classic. I wish you could have seen it before that kid destroyed it. I think we should press charges. I know money isn't a problem, but that child needs to be taught a lesson."

I sat down in my easy chair across the room from the couch. "Susan, we are not going to press charges. As a matter of fact you are going to call the restaurant that the two of you were at and tell them that your boyfriend borrowed it without permission and will be held responsible. Furthermore, I want you to contact the fire department and offer to buy them a new truck, or at least pay to repair their old one. You can take that out of my shares."

She stared at me completely dumbstruck. "We never said anything about a restaurant or how the car was destroyed. And how did you know what color they painted it? You told them to surprise you."

James chimed in with his own concern, "What do you mean I will be held responsible? She borrowed it."

I sat forward in my chair and flipped over the license plate, and completely ignored Susan's inquiry. I turned my attention to James instead. "James, you're not going to be blamed for the car. That's just what we are going to tell the restaurant. Let's just say I'm concerned about that young man's future. As for the rest, the best I can come up with right now is that I saw it in a dream. Now if the two of you are sure you are all right, I would like to return to bed and get some more sleep."

Two weeks later I had an idea how I could get the globe back. With the globe back in my possession I would be able to return to my timeline and get back to the business of fulfilling the promise I made to the genie. The hardest part would be returning the timeline back to the way it was supposed to be. If I was going to stay, I had no problem living like a king and helping Miss Maryweather at the same time. However, if I was going to be returning to my proper time, I would have to find a way to return the timeline to its original state. Come to think of it, I had to return it, or I would have created another time paradox. If I hadn't seen Susan in the military, I would never have recognized her at the restaurant on Battery Point. The dull ache that had plagued me before, when I encountered the first paradox, returned with a vengeance.

I walked into the office, booted up the computer and looked around in confusion. I checked the calendar, Monday, June 4, 2001. It took me a moment to remember that I had given Susan the day off. After a few minutes, I had cashed out all of my stocks and transferred all of my assets, totaling over ninety million dollars, to an off-shore numbered account. I had started that account in case I ever came under investigation for insider trading and now I found that it provided the answer to my paradox. After I verified all of my funds were secure in Switzerland, I called the SEC. I gave them an anonymous tip that the firm Jonson and Maryweather Investments was insider trading and all the proof was in their office. I knew it was a harsh thing to do, and if she ever saw me again...she would punch me in the nose.... Now it all made sense.

After I hung up the phone, I wiped the hard drive of all information that could be used against either myself or Susan. I took one last look around the house, took all the cash and the necklace from the safe in my room, and went out into the garage. In the corner of the first bay was a five gallon gas can. I carried it back to the office, set it on the desk, stuffed a rag into the top, and lit it. I calmly walked out of the house, pausing only once to take a picture off of wall, climbed into one of the various cars I had purchased over the years, and drove into town.

At a costume shop I picked up a fake mustache, a trench coat, a wide brimmed hat, and a fake reporter's badge. My plan for getting the globe back was simple. I would have to go back to when I lost it and simply retrieve it. The hardest part would be getting there, but I remembered where the globe would be in a few days. Or where it had been a few days from now, or... My head started to throb again as it always did when I tried to think my way through a time travel incident.

My cell phone rang. It was Susan and she was more than a little upset.

"David, what's going on? I just checked on the stocks and I saw that you had cashed out everything you had. When I tried to make a trade, all of my assets were frozen! And when I called the SEC to find out why, they told me that we were under investigation for insider trading! And your pulling all of your stocks at once just screams guilty! What am I going to do?"

Her tirade ended in gasping sobs on the other end of the connection. Softly I told her that it would be all right and that, as bad as it got, she shouldn't join the Army. Her sobs came to an abrupt halt as her anger flashed back through her.

"I believe you have been lying to me all these years. You knew my name before you came to my table that day and you used me to make millions. Well, I hope you're happy. I might join the Army just to spite you! Good riddance!"

I imagined her slamming the phone down hard enough to break it, even though all I heard on my end was a subtle click. With that bridge burned and faith in the knowledge that I had pushed her into doing what I remembered she had done, I rolled down my window and tossed out my phone.

Chapter 13
Retrieving The Globe

On the morning of June 11, I dressed up in the costume I had purchased and checked out of the cheap motel I had been hiding in. I climbed into my car and drove to where I knew the globe had been, or would be, sitting unattended for a few moments. I thought back to the last time I had been there. I glanced at myself in the mirror and actually remembered seeing myself there. At six thirty I turned into the parking lot of the Gomez Chicken Plant and parked my car close to the building. I checked my disguise in the mirror once more and stepped out of the car. As I approached the front door, a younger version of myself, in a headless chicken costume, opened the door from the inside.

I flashed my badge to get his attention and said in my most authoritative voice, "David Jonson? I need to ask you a few questions about the incident that happened on the twenty first of May. Is there anywhere we can go to talk in private?"

The color drained from his face and I could imagine the thoughts of that car tumbling through his mind, just like it had in mine since that day. His answer came out as a weak stutter.

"Sh- sh- sure. I need to go back up to the locker room and get my head anyway. I really do forget it since it's not screwed on." His face fell when his attempt at humor failed. Sighing, he led the way through the plant to the main stairwell up to the offices.

As we made our way up the stairs, he began to babble on about how the owner of the Camaro had called and told the restaurant that he wasn't going to be held responsible and that he wouldn't be hearing any more about it. He would have continued to tell me about how the restaurant had fired him anyway, but at that moment he opened the door to the office area and came face to face with someone who obviously didn't belong there. Of course that person was me. Or more specifically, us. For a brief second, we all made eye contact, and then the intruder turned and sprinted toward the back office. The youngest version of myself quickly gave chase, trailing feathers behind him. I caught up with him just as he started to try and break down the door to the supervisor's office. The door started to give under the assault and we heard a loud bang from inside the office. Fire alarms all over the plant started to howl just as the office door flew open.

As the chicken-suited version of me ran to the opened fire escape, I made my way straight to the briefcase sitting on the floor beside the desk. I reached into the outside pocket of the case and grasped the globe. Without hesitation I spun the date on the bottom to April 10, 1996, and left the time set for seven in the morning. I selected Central Park, New York as my destination and with a flash, the office disappeared and I found myself in the center of Times Square. I considered myself lucky. As wildly inaccurate as the globe was, I could have wound up in the harbor.

I flagged down a cab and directed him to the alley where I had been mugged, or would be mugged in five hours. The cabbie dropped me off about a block from my destination, and I crept down the street to the opening of the alley. I looked down the alley and spotted two of the guys that were there when I lost the globe in the first place. Just as I was trying to find a good spot to hide and wait, my pocket vibrated and the muffled voice of the genie demanded my attention. I quickly crept away from the alley to an area where I felt safe pulling out the globe.

"All right, we're in a place I can talk now. What can I do for you, Genie?"

"You, Sir, are not my master. You are the same person, however you are not of the same time. I am assuming that you are aware of the consequences if you do not return me to my proper timeline."

"Listen, I am your master, or else I wouldn't be able to talk to you, right? So let me tell you what happened. In about four and a half hours, I, or at least a younger me, will appear in that alley over there where I will be mugged by four armed men. During that time the younger me will lose a later version of you and be stuck in this time period until the time when I stole you from myself... Am I making any sense at all? If all goes according to plan, when the previous me appears and loses the later you, I will be able to pick up the later you and return the current you to your current me. Did you follow all that?"

"Let me see if I have this straight, Sir. A version of you that is in my future, your past, is going to lose a recent future version of me and spend a little over five years here until he catches up with present me in the timeline. That is who you are now. After you retrieve the near future me, you will use current me to return me back to my current you. Does that sound right?"

"Um, yeah, that about sums it up I guess."

"Have you considered, Sir, that if you fail to return current me to my current you, that you present will cease to exist? If I am not in the briefcase when my current you tries to use me, the timeline will be altered."

I paused for a moment and thought about what the genie had said. I didn't really like the idea of having an existence problem, but if I failed, I guess I would never know anyway. I told the genie that I wouldn't fail and slipped the globe back into my pocket. I crept back to the alley entrance and hid behind a dumpster.

At exactly twelve noon, there was a flash of light and

a younger me was standing there in the middle of the alley. I watched as the four gangsters rose to their feet and started toward him. I watched myself backing slowly away toward the road, and I spotted the pallet that had tripped me up. I saw a smug look cross my younger self's face, only to be replaced with confusion and panic. When the younger me knocked out the ringleader, I had to bite my knuckle to keep from laughing. After a few more steps, he tripped over the pallet and landed flat on his back. The briefcase he was holding hit the ground and the outside pocket burst open, sending the globe rolling across the alley underneath the dumpster I was hiding behind. I picked up the globe and watched as my younger self scrambled to his feet and broke all sorts of personal speed records running away with all four goons in hot pursuit.

I pulled out the first globe and held it in my right hand. "O.K. Genie, I am going to take you back now. I need you to promise that you won't tell the younger me about what is going to happen to him."

The globe I had just retrieved answered first and said, "I did not say a word, Sir."

"Thank you." I replied as I slipped the newly-retrieved globe into my jacket pocket. I turned back to the first globe. "Now to return you to the briefcase from whence you came."

I pointed at the red dot where I had started and said the phrase, "I want to go back to there and then," and with a flash I was standing back in the office behind my feathered self. I slipped the proper globe back into the briefcase and calmly walked out of the offices and down the stairs. When I reached the parking lot, I collected all of the stuff out of my car that I wanted to keep and spun the date on the bottom of the globe till it read August 28, 2006. After I set the date, I had to figure out where I was going to live. I remembered a town one of the guys in my unit said he used to live in. He was always bragging about how beautiful it was. Since I didn't have anywhere else to be, and I really needed to vacate my current location, I set my target destination for Greenville, South Carolina, and with a flash, I was there.

Chapter 14
Present Day

Martin switched off the computer and stood up from the desk. David was sitting on the couch and started to protest, but instantly fell into a coughing fit. When he had recovered enough to continue his objections, Martin silenced him with a single raised finger.

"Sir, the doctor told me to make you rest as much as possible. He would undoubtedly be upset to find that I have let you work this long. We will pick back up tomorrow where we left off. Would you care for some dinner?"

David grumbled for a moment about not being able to find good help before answering. "What are my options?"

"Yes or no."

David stared at Martin for a few moments before letting a grin slowly spread across his elderly face. "You know what? I could really go for a big plate of spaghetti and meatballs."

Martin cleared his throat. "I believe you had that for dinner last night, Sir."

"I did? Are you sure?"

"Quite. And if I remember correctly, the night before that as well."

A look of confusion crossed David's face. "I don't remember having spaghetti last night. I think I would remember eating my favorite meal, especially if I had eaten it two nights in a row."

"No offense, Sir, but I do not think your memory is as sharp as it used to be."

"Nonsense, my memory is as sharp as a tack. Just try me.

"What color are the socks on your feet?"

"Black." David pulled up his pant leg and was surprised to find a white sock on his foot. He glared at his foot for a moment and then at Martin. Martin just shook his head.

"Could I interest you in a nice prime rib? Or perhaps some fresh calamari?"

"The prime rib will be fine, Martin. Thank you."

"As you wish, Sir."

After Martin had left the office to go and prepare the evening meal, David forced himself to his feet and shuffled over to the bookshelf. In the middle of a collection of encyclopedias was a false group of books disguised to look like part of the set, complete with leather bindings, titles, and volume numbers. David removed these books to reveal a small wall safe. He swiftly entered the combination and pulled open the door. Inside the safe was a folder containing his last will and testament and the picture he had rescued from the house he had built during his excursion into the past to get rich. The picture had been taken the day he had moved into that house and was the only picture he had ever had of Susan. She had insisted that there needed to be at least one picture in his new house, and she might as well be in it.

David gathered up the folder and the picture and slowly made his way over to the desk. As he sat down, memories of the time he had spent with Susan flooded through him. He may not have been able to remember the color of the socks he was wearing, but he could recall every detail of the days spent in the past with perfect clarity. A deep sadness overcame him as he thought of the way he had left her. For the past fifty years he had been working with Martin to try and make right the pain and grief he had caused Susan. Every time she was in some kind of financial distress, he would find some way to send money to her, through an odd contest, or even the supposed death of a distant, obscure relative. On her wedding day, he had sent a sizable cash gift in a card signed "from a friend." When her children were born, he sent anonymous gifts to each of them as well, and when they reached college age, he arranged for each of them to receive a full scholarship to any school of their choice. Through the years, he continued to help her family in any way he could but never once revealed who he was. Now that he could see the end approaching, he felt the need to let her know who had been helping her, not to earn her gratitude, but to possibly receive her forgiveness.

Since David didn't have any children of his own, nor had he ever married, he didn't have anyone to put as a beneficiary on his will. Inside the folder with the will was a single, lined sheet of paper with the names of all three of Susan's children and all six of her grandchildren. On the last page of the will was a blank line for him to write in the name of the person or persons who were to receive his estate in the event of his death. Without hesitation he wrote down the names of the six grandchildren. Below the beneficiary section was a space for any additional thoughts, so he jotted down a couple of last instructions for Martin and closed the file. He carefully carried the file and the picture back to the safe, locked the door, and replaced the false books on the shelf. He shuffled his way back to the couch and was just about to sit down when Martin returned to the room.

"Dinner is served, Sir, in the formal dining room. Would you like me to show you the way?"

David just shook his head, and Martin sensed that he wasn't up to his usual playful banter. From the look on David's face he could tell what, or more specifically who, David was thinking about.

"We could call her if you like, Sir. After all these years she may have forgiven you. You really should not keep punishing yourself the way you have been."

"No, Martin. Thanks, but no. When the time comes, I feel certain that she will know everything she needs to know. For now, let's go eat. By the way, what's for dinner?"

Martin looked at David for a second with a puzzled look on his face. "Before I tell you, do you remember what color socks you are wearing?"

Now it was David's turn to look puzzled. "What does the color of my socks have to do with dinner? If you must know, they're black. I always wear black socks."

"Very good, Sir. The main course tonight is spaghetti and meatballs. I have your salad course all set on the table. Now, if you would please follow me."

David smiled, "Oh good, spaghetti. I haven't had spaghetti in months."

Chapter 15
The Journey Begins Again

Greenville, South Carolina, was every bit as beautiful as I had been told it was. I had appeared in a park in the center of the city next to a river that ran through the middle of it. Walking out of the park and onto Main Street, I was greeted with wonderful aromas from various nearby cafés and restaurants. I followed my nose to one such open air café and decided to sit and have lunch. After I finished my lunch, I decided to try and find a place to live. I picked up a local home buyers magazine and flipped through it. Near the back of the magazine at the bottom of the page was a gorgeous mansion sitting on twenty acres of land located in a small town just outside of Greenville. I had never heard of Simpsonville before, so I figured I would take a short tour through the town on my way to have a look at the property. With the rest of the cash that was in my pocket, I rented a car from a nearby rental lot and set out. Driving through Simpsonville was like being transported back in time, from the clock tower on Main Street to the antique police car parked alongside one of the back roads. When I finally pulled up to the front of the house, I knew this was where I wanted to live.

I went to the bank and opened up a new account and transferred ten million from my off shore account into it. When the bank manager asked if there was anything else he could do for me, I just smiled and told him I would be in touch.

I used the rental car's GPS to find my way to the realtor's office. When I pulled up to the office I was greeted by a painfully thin woman in her late thirties with hair that

was obviously not her natural color. She glared at me with
a sour look on her face that made me feel as if I had just
spoiled the rest of her day. That is, until I pointed to the ad
in the magazine and mentioned that I would like to buy the
mansion in Simpsonville at the asking price. The prospect of
such a large sale changed her demeanor drastically. Her face
lit up with the biggest grin I had ever seen. She must have
thought it would put me at ease, but it had quite the opposite
effect. With more than a little worry for the woman's sanity,
I followed her into her office where she had me sign a formal
offer for the property. She called the owners of the house, and
they were thrilled to have a buyer after having their house on
the market for only one week. Since the owners had already
moved out of state, the house was sitting vacant, and they
wanted to close as soon as possible. After a few calls to the
lawyer's office, the closing was set for the following Monday.

One week later I was standing in the entrance to my
new home. The grand entrance hall was made to impress
all who entered. A large oak double staircase led up to the
second floor where a balcony wrapped all the way around
the entrance hall. At the top of the staircase was a large set
of oak doors that led into the sitting room outside the master
suite. All around the balcony on the second floor were doors
leading into six other bedroom suites, three on each side of
the entrance hall. All of the rooms upstairs had thick, lush
carpeting, while the downstairs was all hardwoods. On either
side and also in the back of the entrance hall were large,
frosted glass French doors. The doors on the left led to a
formal sitting room, library, and dining room. The doors on
the right led to an office and a large game room. And the
doors at the back of the entrance hall led into the kitchen.

I walked through the doors into the kitchen. At the back
of the kitchen was a door that led into the four-car garage.
I had chatted with the previous owners for a while and we

talked about how we had each come to make our fortunes. The topic of hobbies came up, and I told them about my restoration projects and of the ill-fated Camaro. They were so moved by my story that they said they would leave a project that the gentleman had just finished on the promise that I wouldn't let my secretary borrow it.

I entered the garage and found a car that was protected by a cloth cover. The cover did a pretty good job of concealing the make and model of the car, but the rims sticking out from under the cover were a dead giveaway. I walked over to the car and threw the cover back revealing sparkling blue paint, white racing stripes, and lots of chrome. I laughed until my sides hurt and tears blurred my vision. Once again I was the proud owner of a 1968 Camaro.

The next few weeks went by in a blur. I spent most of my time trying to find furniture that I liked that would fit the style of the house. When I built the house I had lived in while trapped in the past, Susan had picked everything out. All I had to do was sign the checks and she took care of the rest. I thought about contacting her but I chose instead to keep my distance and help her whenever I could without her knowledge. I didn't think she would trust me, or even talk to me, after what I did to her, and she would undoubtedly be confused after coming face to face with my younger self in the military.

Surprisingly, the office was the easiest room to furnish. Since the room only had one window on the east wall, I decided to line the north wall with floor-to-ceiling shelves and the east wall with shorter shelves under the window. I found a long, overstuffed couch that looked very similar to the one I had in my first office, and I put that against the south wall. The room itself was large enough that I was able to fit a very large antique desk on the east end of the room facing west, toward the door. The layout reminded me of the stereotypical CEO office, and I smiled at the thought.

After I was completely settled in my new home, I once again started on the task of finding and retrieving the missing pieces of the genie's lamp. The next piece on my list was the dragon. The genie had said that it was cast to represent the military prowess of Genghis Khan. It gave the person who held it the same strength and courage that Khan had wished for. He had also mentioned that the servant had hidden it in the Forbidden City. After consulting with the genie, we agreed that a good place to start looking for a golden dragon with mystical powers would be the Palace Museum in Beijing.

I packed my bags, grabbed my passport, and made my way to the airport. I could have used the globe to jump straight there, but I felt the risk of appearing somewhere inappropriate and causing an international incident was too great. Besides I was starting to believe that all that jumping around was having some negative effects on my health. I had asked the genie about it once, and he assured me that it was a figment of my imagination, but that didn't make me any less uneasy with the concept. I found myself agreeing more and more with a doctor I had seen on a popular sci-fi TV show. He had also had a severe aversion to having his molecules scrambled every time he had to go somewhere.

"What doctor would that be, Sir?"

"C'mon, Martin. Surely you know who I'm talking about. McCoy, Martin, I was referring to McCoy. You know, Leonard H. All these years we have been together and you don't know anything about my favorite show."

"Some of us actually work around the house, Sir."

"Speaking of work…let's get back to it, shall we?"

"As you wish."

After two hours of airport security lines and searches I began to rethink my position on using the globe. It would have been very easy to just step out of line and jump straight to Beijing, however, I had packed the globe with my checked luggage in order to avoid any unnecessary questions when my carry-on was searched.

After a relatively short hop on a regional jet to Newark, New Jersey, I boarded a Continental Airlines Boeing 747 for the last leg of my journey. I made my way into the first class compartment, found my seat, and had a look around. There were only two other people sitting in first class. One was a fairly small, wealthy-looking young man in an expensive business suit. He was seated two rows behind me and staring absentmindedly out the right side of the plane. The other gentleman was a gorilla of a man seated in the back of the compartment. He didn't look like the type of person who would typically buy a first class ticket, but, judging by the look of him, he didn't get a free upgrade with his charming personality. If there was an air marshal on board, that man would be my first guess. Everything about him screamed agent, from his dark sunglasses and thick mustache to his cheap gray suit and patent leather shoes.

The flight attendant interrupted my observations of my fellow passengers with her pre-flight safety briefing. She droned on about how to fasten and remove the seat belt, the proper use of the oxygen mask, and where we could find our flotation devices. All of which I felt was quite superfluous since our flight plan had us traveling over the North Pole. If we did have some kind of emergency landing I didn't think any of us would make it. Between drowning, freezing to death, or being eaten by some creature or other, I didn't feel confident in our chances.

The first few hours of the flight were uneventful, and I even managed to get some sleep. Three hours after takeoff,

I was awakened by a shrill, high-pitched scream. I turned
in my seat to see the gorilla cowering against the window
with the other first-class passenger standing over him with a
gun. I looked around for something I could use as a weapon,
but there was nothing to be found. My frantic search drew
the attention of the gunman, and he turned toward me and
leveled his gun. As I raised my hands an idea came to mind.

"You don't want to shoot me. It would be hazardous to
your health." I was grateful that my voice wasn't shaking
near as bad as my knees were.

"Don't you mean that it would be hazardous to *your*
health? I believe I am the one holding the gun." As he
finished his statement he took two steps forward and I
couldn't help but notice his thick Irish accent.

I lowered my hands before answering, "The pistol you
are currently holding is a nine-millimeter Glock, am I right?
If you fire that weapon, the bullet has a fairly good chance of
passing clean through me and continuing on through the wall
behind me, and do you know what is on the other side of that
wall?"

The hijacker stopped moving toward me and thought
for a second. The gorilla took advantage of his momentary
distraction and snuck out of the compartment and made his
way back to the stewardess station. The gunman turned and
watched the big guy leave and then turned back to me.

"There is nothing on the other side of that wall. So it
wouldn't hurt anything to shoot you, would it?"

I started to explain explosive decompression and the
negative effects on the health of everyone aboard, but he
apparently didn't want to hear it and pulled the trigger. The
round passed through the center of my chest, exited out my
back and proceeded out through nose of the plane. A low
whistling noise filled the compartment as the front of the
plane started to tear itself apart. Just before the darkness

closed in around me, I felt the floor drop away and I could see daylight as I was sucked out along with the entire first class compartment.

With a start I woke up. I was still alive, and still safely in my seat. I felt my chest and, aside from being soaked with sweat, it was whole and in perfect condition. I had seen enough of those movies with the doomed teenagers to know a premonition when I had one, so I knew I had to act fast. I stood up and made my way back to the small man on the right side of the plane.

"I know what you are planning, and it won't work. It will result in all of our deaths, and I will not allow that to happen."

The man looked at me with a mix of confusion and concern. "I beg your par–"

He never finished his sentence. I leaned in across the vacant seat between us and drove my fist into his jaw as hard as I could. The man's eyes rolled back in his head, and I drew back to let him have another, but before I could deliver, my whole body went stiff and the world went dark.

I came to and found myself tied to my seat with the gorilla standing in front of me. He looked even more disagreeable than when I had first seen him. When he noticed that I was awake, he cracked his knuckles, placed his hands on the armrests of my seat, and leaned in close. He had removed his sunglasses, and I could feel his intense gaze trying to bore through my head. If his death glare didn't kill me then his breath probably would. It was bad enough that I felt confident it could peel the paint off the outside of the aircraft.

When he was certain that he had my attention, he spoke a single word. "Why?" His voice was not the high-pitched, girly voice I had heard in my dreams. It was more of a deep, resonating, authoritative boom that demanded immediate obedience. I didn't think I could use the Klingon language to get out of this one, so I tried a new tactic.

"Why what?" As bad as I was feeling, it nearly sounded like Klingon anyway. I was still suffering from the effects of whatever he had used to knock me out. My mouth was dry, and every muscle in my body ached as though I had been beaten with a baseball bat. The big guy obviously didn't like my answer. He removed his jacket and started to roll up his sleeves, exposing forearms as big as my thighs. His attempt at intimidating me was, to say the least, successful. So I decided to come clean and tell him everything. Well, maybe not everything. I left out the part of my dream where he screamed like a little girl and ran away.

The big guy, Carlos, turned out to actually be an air marshal, and he had used a Taser on the back of my neck to subdue me. The other gentleman was a banker from Great Britain who seemed to take everything in stride after I explained it to him and even accepted my apology–just before catching me with a right hook and sending me, yet again, into unconsciousness.

Chapter 16
Beijing

The rest of the flight was uneventful, mainly because I was unconscious. After I made my way through customs, I flagged down a taxi and proceeded to murder the Chinese language in an effort to tell the driver which hotel I was staying at. The driver just chuckled and shook his head. After several failed attempts to pronounce anything intelligent, the driver finally raised his hand to stop me.

"Listen, bub, I don't know if you even bothered to look at me since you climbed into my cab, but I'm not from here. I speak English just fine. So, where to?"

I apologized and told him the name of the hotel where I had reservations, and after a short drive we arrived at the Peninsula Hotel. The hotel itself was excellent, from the accommodations to the world class service, but the thing that made it perfect was its proximity to the Forbidden City.

The next morning, I left my hotel room and walked the short distance to Tiananmen Square and entered the Forbidden City through the South Gate. A tour of the city was just starting, so I slipped in with the crowd in hopes of learning something. There seemed to be a sampling of every type of tourist, from the overweight couple clad in flowery Hawaiian shirts to the geek with the pocket protector, thick glasses, and overused notebook. There was also a very harried and frazzled single mom with a six-year-old son who had to know everything. I felt certain that by the end of the tour everyone would know that child's name. Every two or three minutes his mother could be heard saying something like, "Not now, Jake." or "Jake, if you will just listen you might learn something." My favorite was when she told him he would learn more with his mouth shut and ears open.

The tour was actually very informative. I learned that construction had started in the year 1406 under Emperor YongLe. I had known that Emperor YongLe had built the Forbidden City, but I hadn't known when. Every part of the city had been planned, right down to the last detail; even the direction the buildings faced had a significance. According to the guide, everything bad that had happened to China was believed to have come from the north, from the cold winter winds to enemy invasions, so they built every single pavilion facing south, except the ones for the rejected concubines.

Our tour wound around the city, visiting every pavilion in order of importance, from least to greatest. The guide said you could tell the significance of a building by the number of animal statues on its roof, the more it had the greater its importance. The building with the most statues was the Hall of Supreme Harmony or Taihe Dian. The building itself was massive, standing just over 122 feet tall, 122 feet long, almost 209 feet wide, and it was built on top of a nearly 23-foot-high marble terrace. This was the hall where the grandest of ceremonies were held–everything from a new Emperor's ascension to the throne to the celebration of the Winter Solstice. My interest in this hall was mostly that it was where all of the generals were dispatched to war.

The tour guide was still rattling off her well-rehearsed speech as we walked into the hall when Jake raised his hand.

"Excuse me, ma'am, but how many dragons are there in here?"

The tour guide chuckled before answering, "Young man, you are not the first person to ask that very question. Up until a few years ago I didn't know the answer either, so I came in on my day off and counted them all. Does anyone have a guess?"

The young man who had asked the question raised

his hand, and after being acknowledged by the guide said, "Three hundred?"

The guide shook her head. "Not even close. There are 12,694 dragons that are either painted, carved, or cast. My favorites are the ones on the ceiling playing with the pearl. The pearl is called the 'Xuanyuan Mirror.' It is said that they can tell right from wrong, and are even able to determine if someone doesn't belong on the throne. Legend has it that anyone taking the throne who was not a descendant of the Emperor Huang Di would be struck dead by the pearl falling from the ceiling. This legend was so powerful that in 1916, after Emperor PuYi was forced to abdicate his throne, the man who tried to make himself the next Emperor, Yuan Shikai, had the throne moved out from under the pearl."

I raised my hand and was acknowledged by the guide. "I noticed that the throne is roped off. Is there any way that I could get a closer look at it? I am very interested in the carvings on the throne itself."

The guide shook her head, "I'm afraid the throne is off limits to the public. Now, are there any more questions?"

The same little boy who asked about the dragons raised his hand. "What happened to the man who tried to make himself Emperor? Did the pearl fall on him? How did they get it back up there? Did he die of mysterious causes? Was he assassinated? Did he–"

Before he could say any more his mother put her hand on his shoulder and told him to take a breath. The guide smiled and shook her head.

"As you can see, the pearl didn't fall on him. He wasn't poisoned either, neither was he assassinated. Barely a year and a half after he took the throne as Emperor, Yuan Shikai died from uremia. However, had he not succumbed to an illness, he would probably not have lasted much longer anyway, as his closest supporters and his military warlords had started to turn against him. But that is a story for another time. If you would kindly follow me…"

The guide turned and walked out of the hall, and the rest of the group obediently followed. I pretended to be interested in the carvings on one of the various pillars in the room while I waited for them to leave. As the group left the building, I heard the little boy ask his mother what uremia was, but they were too far away for me to hear the answer she gave him.

After I was sure they were gone, I made my way back to the throne. I had read a little on the emperors of China, trying to find where the Dragon Piece had gone, but I didn't have any theories until the guide told us about Yuan Shikai losing the support of his military warlords. Since the dragon was cast to represent Khans fierceness in battle and military prowess, and the genie had said that it was hidden in the Forbidden City, I could only guess that it was hidden near, or possibly in, the Dragon Throne. When she said that after Yuan Shikai named himself emperor, he had the throne moved and then lost all his military support, I realized that not only had the Dragon Piece been in the throne, but someone must have known about it and removed it in order to keep Yuan Shikai from abusing its powers.

I took one last look around and ducked under the red velvet rope that was all the way around the throne and its platform. It didn't take me long to locate a small, rectangular hole on the inside of the left armrest. The hole was perhaps four inches long, three inches tall, and two inches deep. Not surprisingly, there was nothing in the small space, however there was a very peculiar set of marks all around the outside of it.

-.. .- - . / ... - — .-.. . -. / .— .- -. ... .- . .-. -.- / .—
... - / .— —. . .— -....

The pattern repeated itself three times around the outside of the hole and looked to be part of the original design of the throne, but something seemed familiar about the pattern. I heard another tour group approaching so I snapped a picture with my camera and jumped off the throne.

Later that evening, after I had returned to my hotel room, I studied the image saved on my camera and tried to figure out the pattern. I was drawing a complete blank until out of sheer boredom I started tapping out the pattern with a pencil. The pattern was Morse Code! I ventured down to the lobby of the hotel and found a computer and logged on to the Internet. After a few minutes of searching, I found a site that had all the Morse Code translations. I printed out a copy and made my way back to my room. I sat down at the desk and started to translate the message. Dash, dot, dot...that was a *D*. Dot, Dash...an *A*. Next was a *T* and then an *E*. I felt like Ralph in *A Christmas Story* when he received his Little Orphan Annie decoder ring. The next word started with an *S*, followed by *T, O, L, E,* and *N*. My hands started to shake in anticipation as I wrote out the final translations, *January 1, 1916. Date stolen January 1, 1916.*

I thought back to the presentation the tour guide had given in the throne room. 1916 was the year the throne was moved out from under the pearl, and I was willing to bet that wasn't the only change that was being made to the Palace in preparation for the new Emperor. A plan started to form in my mind. With the right equipment, I believed I could infiltrate the Forbidden City and steal the dragon piece.

I removed the globe from my suitcase and selected my home as my destination. After a brief flash I realized, when I found myself in Southside Park almost six miles from my house, that I hadn't made any jumps from my new home yet.

The next morning I woke up bright and early and
packed a backpack with a few things I had been collecting in
preparation for another journey into the past. Having learned
a very valuable lesson from my first foray into history, I
decided that taking a few essential items would be prudent.
First, I packed an incredibly bright flashlight, one capable
of blinding an opponent if caught by surprise. Next, I threw
in a Taser just in case I needed to subdue someone. I toyed
with the idea of adding a tranquilizer gun, but all I had was
the rifle version, so I threw in a can of pepper spray instead. I
walked out into the garage and opened up the box that I kept
all of my camping gear in and removed a coil of rope and
a survival knife. While I was out there, I also found my old
canteen which I washed and filled with water.

I also needed to change my clothes. My current attire,
which consisted of a pair of tan dress slacks and a collared
shirt, would probably not help me very much in my endeavor.
Instead, I opted for a set of black fatigues and combat boots.
I strapped my survival knife on my hip and reached for
the globe. I spun the rings on the bottom, setting the date
for January 1, 1916, zero one hundred hours. Just before I
selected my destination, I had a funny thought and walked
into the kitchen and started digging through my junk drawer.
After a few seconds of searching, I found a laser pointer and
a roll of duct tape which I added to my bag.

Once again I held the globe in my hands, took one last
look around my house, selected my destination, and with a
flash I was thrown into the past.

Chapter 17
The Dragon Piece

For a brief moment I found myself falling before landing in the top of a tree. After the disorientation that came after every jump passed, I consulted the genie to find out why I was sixty feet off the ground.

"Sir, do you remember what you selected as your destination?"

I thought for a moment before answering, "I selected the location of the Peninsula Hotel, but that doesn't explain why I am in the top of this tree."

"The location you selected was your departure point when you jumped home, correct? When you made that jump, you were in your room on the eighth floor, and you appeared in the exact location you left from."

"You do, however, realize that if you kill me, whether accidentally or on purpose, I won't be able to help you anymore." Before the genie could answer, I placed the globe in my backpack and began to extract myself from the tree. When I reached the ground, I started to make my way to the Forbidden City, staying in the shadows as much as I could. The first major obstacles I would have to overcome were the exterior wall and the moat. The wall was ten meters tall and the moat was fifty meters wide. On top of the wall at each corner was a guard tower, and unlike days of old when they had bows and arrows, these soldiers all had rifles in their hands.

I was just about to dive into the moat and attempt to swim across when I noticed a fairly large group of people heading toward the south gate. With all the work that went on to make the palace ready for the new Emperor, it didn't surprise me to find that they worked around the clock. It was actually a kind of relief, because it would make gaining entry that much easier.

I dropped my backpack behind a nearby bush, snuck up behind the last person in the group, and tried to pull off one of those moves I had seen in the movies–the one where the hero grabs an individual and drags him off and steals his clothes without raising any alarms. This technique does not work. Everything went great, right up until I actually grabbed the worker. As soon as my hands made contact, the man spun around, and like a scene from an old kung-fu flick, proceeded to whip my tail all over the street. The man beat me so badly that he didn't even call for the palace guards; he just left me there to writhe in agony and shame.

I picked up what was left of my pride and retrieved my bag from its hiding spot. I decided I wouldn't make the same mistake twice and pulled out the Taser. After only fifteen or twenty minutes of waiting, another group of workers approached my position, heading for the south gate. The last man in line was about my size, wearing a large hooded cloak, and struggling to push a cart full of supplies and large clay pots. Every now and then someone in the line would turn and yell something back at the man, he would wave them off, and the whole group would laugh and move on. After the entire group passed, I started after the man with the cart and was just about to knock him out with the Taser when he stopped and looked back at me. What I saw under the hood froze me in my tracks. Instead of the tired and worn face of a local worker, I was confronted by a Caucasian male with black hair and piercing blue eyes. The man glared at me and then noticed the Taser in my hand. He shook his head and nodded toward the bushes where I had been hiding. When we were safely out of sight of the guards and other workers, he threw his hood back and started to throw all sorts of accusations at me.

"Gor Blimey, I just got here! I know MI6 wants results now, but sending someone to take me out of the game is not the fastest way to go about achieving their goals! I realize that I am two days late reporting in, but this *is* my first real field assignment. Besides, how do they expect me to complete my mission if they don't give me the newest gadgets to work with?" He gestured to the unused Taser in my hand.

I thought up a quick story before answering him. "Listen, Bud, the reason MI6 didn't give you one of these is because they don't have them yet. I am with the CIA and I am just as surprised as you are. What are you doing here anyway?"

His reaction was priceless. "You're a Yank! I should have known in that outfit. If you didn't expect to find me, why are *you* here? And what is this CIA you said you are with?"

A brief lesson from one of my high school government classes came flooding to the surface of my memory. I had been flirting with a young woman sitting next to me and not paying the least bit of attention to the teacher when he decided to direct a question my way. *Mr. Jonson, since you know this material so well that you don't see the need to pay attention in my class, maybe you could tell us when the CIA was formed? I will give you a hint, the answer in not on Miss Hawkins' face.* I had done what millions of students had done throughout history, that is, I stuttered and looked completely lost until he pointed at the date he had written on the board. September 18, 1947. Thirty-one years *after* the date where I currently was. I started to panic before suddenly remembering a little bit more from that class. I smiled and stretched the truth just a bit more.

"The CIA is affiliated with the ONI. And as for my mission, I am searching for an ancient artifact that we believe would be better off not falling into the hands of the new emperor."

The MI6 agent looked at me a bit skeptically. "The Office of Naval Intelligence is concerned with ancient Chinese artifacts? Whatever for?"

"If you look back through Chinese history, you will notice that every emperor has had incredible leadership ability when it came to using the military, but only when the orders were given from here. Specifically, when they were seated on the Dragon Throne. This artifact is kept in the arm of that throne. Anyone enlisted in the Emperor's army would find it hard, if not impossible, to resist orders given by their leader while he was in possession of that artifact."

After a few minutes of silent contemplation, he seemed to accept my story and relief flooded through me. In the distance we heard the rumble of the large gate being closed. He took a small watch out of his pocket and checked the time.

"Blast! They won't open that gate again for another four hours and that's our only way in. We'll just have to wait until then to gain access."

I sat down and pulled out my canteen. "You still haven't told me why you are here, or even what your name is."

The young agent smiled at me, "The name is James– "

"Bond?"

"No, it's Royceston. I've never heard of anyone by the name of Bond..."

I waved him off and kicked myself for using a movie reference. "Never mind. So, why are you here?"

James sat down and I passed him my canteen. He took a swallow before answering. "Several months ago we determined that the new emperor doesn't have the best of intentions. He is planning to try and expand China's borders again, so I am here to take care of the situation, permanently."

I stared at him in disbelief. "You think you can just walk in and take care of him? What are you planning to do, shoot him? Are you completely out of your mind?! The fallout from such an act could start anoth–"

He put his finger to his lips to get me to quiet down. "We're not as brazen as you Yanks are." He pulled a small vile out of his pocket. "This liquid is a highly concentrated toxin that attacks the kidneys of its victim. Our chemical research division has tailored it to work as slowly as possible. All I have to do is apply it to something that he will come into contact with within twenty-four hours and it will be absorbed through his skin and into his blood stream."

I looked at the clear liquid swishing around in the vial. "Just how long does it take to work? Hours? Days? Weeks?"

"The first test subject took six months to die, but that was a large dose. The Emperor may live as long as a year with this amount. We don't necessarily want him to die right away. We need him to lose support from his followers, and one of the side effects from this drug is loss of mental acuity."

I immediately saw a flaw in his plan. "It won't matter if he still has the artifact. Nobody will be able to question his orders, and that could be even more disastrous. I'll tell you what, we can either go our separate ways and hope that neither one of us get captured and gives the other away, or we could work together. I will help you deliver the poison, and you can help me gain entry into the throne room." I stuck out my hand and he reluctantly took it.

Four hours later we heard the rumble of the south gate being opened. James slipped back into his disguise and motioned for me to climb into his cart.

"Don't you think the guards will search your cart when we try to go through the gate?"

James shook his head and pointed to the side of the cart. "You see those markings? Loosely translated it means latrine digger. That's why all the other workers were pointing and laughing at me. Being made to dig the loo is a punishment for the disgraced in this society–petty thieves, deserters, peeping toms, etc. While you are punished you are considered a lower class of person than any other, and as such you are generally ignored. Even palace guards turn their noses up and their eyes away when you approach. It has turned out to be a wonderful gap in their security."

"So you are posing as a person that digs holes for latrines? How is that any different than someone who digs trenches?"

"Latrine diggers don't dig new latrines... They clean out the old ones and put the waste into these large clay pots. The pots are then taken to the gardens, and the contents are mixed with other compost to make fertilizer. You don't have to worry though, none of these tools have been used for that purpose. So get in."

I shook my head and thought that this Brit was going to have a good time telling his buddies back home about how he was able to talk a Yank into hiding in a cart full of toilet brushes. I climbed in near the middle of the cart, between some of the clay pots, and James piled several coils of rope and a fair number of hand tools on top of me. He claimed that the tools were unused, however my nose was telling me different.

I felt the cart start to rumble forward, and after what seemed like an eternity it came to a stop. I was just about to start extricating myself from the cart when I heard the gruff voice of an imperial guard. I thought for sure our cover was blown until I heard James answer back in flawless Mandarin. I heard a dull thud followed by the sound of someone falling down. A few breathless seconds later, I heard the guard laugh and walk away. After another minute or two of silence the cart started moving again.

When the cart finally came to a halt I was relieved to hear James' voice. "Come on Yank. Let's get this over with."

I extracted myself from the cart and tried to brush what I hoped was just dirt off of my clothes. I slung my bag over my shoulder and asked what had happened when we stopped the first time.

James rubbed his left leg for a minute before replying. "Bloody thug. Not everyone looks away from the lower class. When we got to the gate, he asked me what my crime was, so I told him I was a pickpocket. He decided he needed to add to my punishment by kicking me in the leg."

I looked around and noticed that the sun was starting to brighten the sky around us. "I think we need to get a move on, it's starting to get light out here, and we don't want to get caught wandering around. If anyone ever finds out that you aren't what you appear to be, we will truly be in the fecal matter."

James chuckled and replied, "We have a saying in the agency, *'Semper in excretia, sumus solim profundum variat!'* That's Latin for, 'We're always in the manure, only the depth varies.' "

"I think I have heard that phrase before...." I glanced around the small alley where we had stopped and tried to guess which buildings we were behind. It was amazing how much time could change things. Since nothing looked familiar, I turned back to James. "So, where are we?"

He pulled out a crude, hand drawn map of the city and pointed to a row of buildings just to the East of the South Gate. "We are right here. If we follow this wall north, it will lead us to a small hut that we can hide out in until nightfall."

We started to walk, and I stared at him in disbelief. "If we can't make a move until tonight, why on Earth did we come in here so early? Why didn't we wait until the first shift was coming in tonight?"

"That's easy, the guards are more apt to notice something out of place early in their shift. Since we came in close to the end of their watch, nobody noticed your shoe sticking out the side of the cart. Of course, I would have been in here four hours ago had I not run into you and missed that opportunity. Ah, here we are."

Agent Royceston opened up a door that appeared to be on the back side of a small hut in the northern most part of the city. I looked around and noticed that it was the only building with a door that faced north. I pointed this fact out to James and he snickered.

"This city was built on the premise that nothing good comes from the north. And that belief was well grounded, what with all the winter weather coming in from the north as well as quite a few invading armies. So all the buildings face south, looking toward everything good in the world. Except for this building. This is where the Emperor housed the concubines who had fallen out of favor."

I shook my head, "I think I've heard that before, too."

James pulled his cart over next to another that appeared to have some construction supplies piled on it then ushered me inside the building.

"So," I said as I pulled up a pile of what I hoped was clean linen, "What made you join Her Majesty's Secret Service?"

"It's officially known as the Secret Service Bureau, and I joined to serve the crown like my father before me and to find some answers."

I waited for him to explain and when he didn't I asked, "What kind of answers?"

He seemed to get a far-off look on his face like he was recalling something from his distant childhood. "When I was a boy, my father, Captain Benjamin Royceston, told me of the time he was working in India restoring a Buddhist Temple in the year 1883. He said there was a strange young man that just showed up one day and started poking around claiming to be an American reporter. The American's story didn't add up so my father decided to report him to the Director-General. The next part I thought was a little far-fetched. He would blame it on the heat and the long days working on the temple, but he claims that the American forced him to help him find something in the temple. And the strangest part was that after they found it, he told my father to say 'Hi' to his son James, and then vanished into thin air."

"Why was that the strangest part? Had your father not told him about you?"

"How could he? That was two years before I was born." We sat in silence for a few minutes before he continued. "I don't believe anyone could vanish into thin air, and if there was anyone who could, they could do some serious damage to a rival country's house of government. I don't know why anyone would want to infiltrate a Buddhist temple that was in ruins, unless it was a test run for you Americans to see if you could do it. That was round about the time your ONI started up, was it not?"

I shook my head and tried my best to put his mind at ease. "I don't know of any official operations into India during that time, however, I can tell you that it wasn't an ONI operation. Even though we were founded in March of 1882, we really didn't get rolling until we declared war on Spain in 1898."

After what seemed like days, the sun finally started to disappear behind the western wall, and we crept out of our hiding place. As we walked along the alleyways of the city, I started to wonder if my secret agent friend actually knew where we were going. He never once looked at his map, but instead appeared to be looking at the sky to get his bearings. After only twenty or so minutes, I was hopelessly lost and was willing to wager that James was as well.

I stopped walking and voiced my concerns. "You don't have a clue where we are, do you?"

He gave me a puzzled look and replied, "You can tell what the buildings are by the creatures on top of them. I would have thought an agent of the ONI would have studied his target city. To answer your question, I know exactly where we are. If you haven't noticed, I have been trying to lead us around all of the work details, in an attempt to get us to the throne room without being noticed. Unfortunately, there is a large amount of work being done to the stairway leading up to the throne room. We are going to be hard-pressed to make it past all those workers and guards."

I smiled and took off my backpack. "I think what we need is a distraction. And I happen to have just the thing." I reached into my bag and removed the laser pointer.

Royceston snickered, "The pen is mightier than the sword, eh?"

"This is not your typical pen. It is the most technically advanced distraction device ever created." I aimed the laser just beyond the workers to the base of the top stair and turned it on. The little red dot glowed bright against the stone tile and quickly caught the attention of one of the workers. The worker stopped what he was doing and tapped the shoulder of the man next to him. That worker turned to look at what the first was pointing at and in turn tapped the man next to him. This continued all the way around the group until the entire assembly of workers was staring at the glowing dot. The four guards who were standing at the top of the stairs sensed that something was amiss, and one of them came to investigate. Just as he started down the stairs I swung the laser over to the eastern edge of the staircase as if it were alive and trying to avoid the approaching soldier. Every head in the work detail snapped to the right to follow the glowing dot, much like a cat would in the same situation, which caused the guard to pause on the top step. Slowly, I brought the laser back toward the guard on the top step, dragging the intense stares of the workers with it. Just before it reached his foot, the guard caught sight of the blazing spot, panicked, screamed like a little girl, and tripped over his own feet trying to get away from it.

As the guard fell, I made the laser "run" up his pant leg, which made him scream even louder. The workers all moved in on the guard in order to help drive away the evil glowing spirit attacking him, and the other guards moved in to protect their colleague from what appeared to them as an uprising against the military. The ensuing riot proved to be so effective that Agent Royceston and I were able to walk up the stairs and into the throne room unchallenged.

When we were safely inside, James stopped me and asked, "What was that thing?"

"You mean this?" I held out the laser pointer and he eagerly took it from me. I showed him how to use it and cautioned him not to shine it into his eyes or mine.

"I have never seen such a thing! Oh, the boys back home would love to tear this apart and see what makes it tick."

I retrieved the pointer from him and shook my head. "Your boys will have to wait. Since this is new technology, you can very well imagine that it's expensive. I can't afford to replace this one, however, when we are finished here I will see what I can do to get one sent over to your department."

"I guess they will have to wait, then."

Quietly we crept deeper into the Hall of Supreme Harmony. When we entered the throne room, I was surprised to see that there was nobody there. I had expected to find at least two or three guards keeping a watchful eye on all the priceless artifacts in the room, but there was nobody there at all. The sound of guards running through the building caught my attention, and I realized that the riot I had started earlier had spread further than I had hoped, and every available guard was being called in to regain order.

I walked over to the throne and looked on the inside of the left armrest. Nestled in the small rectangular hole was a beautifully crafted golden dragon. As soon as I touched the dragon, I an immense feeling of self confidence washed over me. I drew my knife and started to etch the Morse code message that had sent me to this time. When James saw what I was doing, he immediately moved to stop me, but before he could even get close I told him to go check on the situation outside. The power of the dragon piece made my suggestion an irresistible order, and he turned on his heel and made his way to the entrance. After James left, I placed the dragon piece in my bag and finished etching the message.

By the time he returned, I had finished my message and had determined the best place to plant the poison. I asked for and received the bottle from James and poured the entire contents into the compartment where the dragon piece had been kept. When the new Emperor sat down on the throne, he would, without a doubt, stick his hand into the small rectangular opening and in doing so, put his hand into the puddle of clear liquid, sealing his fate.

"OK, James, that should just about do it. How did it look outside?"

"That little gizmo of yours has started quite an uprising. Almost all of the workers have turned on the guards, and it's only a matter of time before the order is given to use deadly force. The only reason there hasn't been any gunfire yet is because the roving guards don't carry firearms around the workers for just this instance. If the workers get the upper hand, the soldiers in the towers have orders to open fire until order is restored, which usually means they will shoot until everything that is not in uniform is dead."

I scratched my head for a minute trying to decide how best to proceed. I could have just used the globe and jumped straight home from there, but that would have left James stuck behind enemy lines doubting his sanity. After a minute or two, I came up with a plan and retrieved a couple items out of my bag, one of which was the can of pepper spray. The other was my Taser.

"What kind of contraption is this?" James asked as he took the Taser out of my hand. He turned it over a couple times inspecting it. It was an older model that looked like a bent television remote control with two electrodes protruding from one end.

"That, my friend, is called a Taser. It's yet another technologically advanced piece of gear the boys at R&D let me borrow for this trip." I carefully took the Taser away from James.

"But what does it do?"

"It will make a grown man lay down on the floor and cry if he is unfortunate enough to get hit by it, trust me." Unconsciously I rubbed my right thigh where I had gotten zapped once before.

"Sir, if I may ask, why were you rubbing your leg? I thought you were Tased in the back of the neck, not on your leg. I do not believe I have ever heard of any instance other than that time on the plane."

"It was just before I went back to retrieve the dragon piece. When I was gathering all of the stuff I thought I might need in the past, I thought it might be a good idea to keep the Taser where I could get ahold of it quickly, so I put it in my right pocket. When I walked into the kitchen to get the laser pointer, I bumped into the corner of the counter top on the

island, and the Taser discharged into my thigh. I spent a good five minutes on the floor before I was able to get up and put it in my bag. I didn't think it was prudent information to put in the book, so I just said I put it in my bag to begin with."

"I see, Sir. You are wanting to avoid unnecessary embarrassment by not telling the world that you did not know how to safely carry your Taser."

"Yes, Martin, and if you know what's good for you, that bit of information won't leave this room. Now let's get back to the book."

"As you wish."

We made our way outside and managed to stick to the shadows for a short time. We had actually made it past the majority of the fighting when our luck ran out. One of the guards spotted us trying to escape and came after us bringing one of his companions with him. The two of them caught up with us when we were within just a few yards of the South Gate. The bigger of the two tackled Agent Royceston, and the two of them fell to the ground in a tangle of arms and legs. Before I could be of any assistance, the smaller one attacked me. We hit the ground hard, and I was able to roll away and jump back up to my feet.

Between the two of us, I definitely had the size advantage, whereas the diminutive guard had the upper hand when it came to speed. We circled each other for a few seconds before I remembered that I was still holding the pepper spray and the Taser. I aimed the can at him and depressed the small trigger, sending a stream of irritating fluid directly into his face. In my mind, I had envisioned that a person who had been shot with pepper spray would be instantly blinded, clawing at his eyes and altogether useless in a fight. This was not the case with the little Royal Guard. The more I sprayed him, the angrier he became. Over the

course of just a few seconds, I had completely emptied the
contents of the can, covering nearly half of his body, while
simultaneously dodging multiple punches, kicks, and even
the occasional ball of spit. When I ran out of the spray, the
guard lunged at me, and I instinctively brought the Taser
up to his chest and pressed the button. Once again I was
surprised by the reaction of my foe. Whereas I imagined all
of his muscles contracting causing him to fall to the ground,
he erupted into a huge fireball, ran screaming through the
open South Gate, and dove into the moat. Apparently, pepper
spray is flammable. The other guard and James paused in
their fight to watch the human torch dive off the bridge into
the water, and then both of them turned their gaze back to me.
I pointed the Taser at the big guard and pressed the button
again, making a blue arc jump from electrode to electrode.
The color immediately drained from the poor man's face, and
he ran screaming back into the city, presumably to get help.
James and I didn't stick around long enough to find out.

Once we were safely outside the city walls, I turned to
James and stuck out my hand. "Agent Royceston, it has been
and honor and a pleasure working with you."

James took my proffered hand and shook it firmly.
"Same to you, Sir. If you are ever in or around London, feel
free to come visit me in my office. The ONI shouldn't have
any trouble getting you the contact information. Just be sure
to bring some of those gadgets with you."

"Sure thing. Well, until then..." I turned and walked
away from James, knowing full well that I would never see
him again. I stopped just long enough to pick up an antique
paper fan that was lying on a vendor table near the street.
The vendor was nowhere to be found, I assumed he had
gone to the aid of the flaming guard in the moat. I took one
last glance over my shoulder to make sure I wasn't being
followed and ducked down into an alleyway out of sight of

any prying eyes to make the jump home. After rummaging through my bag for a few seconds, I retrieved the globe, found the marker for my house, spoke the mantra, and with a flash I was back in my living room on September 21, 2006.

Chapter 18
Present Day

Martin turned off the computer and retrieved a blanket from the linen closet in the hall. Mr. Jonson had fallen asleep on the couch, and he carefully covered him up. The large grandfather clock in the corner told him it was only four in the afternoon, but the doctor had said for Mr. Jonson to get lots of rest, and Martin wasn't about to go against the doctor's orders by waking him up. Instead, he used the time to finish his daily chores around the house. First, he cleaned the upstairs. The guest rooms hadn't had any occupants for several years, other than himself, and mainly just needed a good dusting. Next was the master suite. After collecting all of the discarded clothing, making the bed, and vacuuming the carpet, he moved on to the master bath.

When he had finished cleaning upstairs, he checked the time and realized that almost two hours had passed. He went back into the office to check on his boss, and walked in just in time to catch him putting the false books over the safe back on the shelf. David was wheezing heavily and looking very unstable on his feet. Martin moved to his side in the blink of an eye.

"How was your nap, Sir?"

David did his best to wave Martin off, but lacked the strength to even raise his hand. "It would have been better if you hadn't insisted on using that ancient vacuum cleaner. I swear the neighbors are going to start complaining about the noise soon."

Martin shook his head. "Sir, there is no way the neighbors can hear the vacuum from their house. They did not even hear it when you drove your prized Camaro through the back wall of the garage."

"Martin, that was almost ten years ago! Are you ever going to let me live that down?" David collapsed back onto the couch.

"Just as long as you never ask to drive again."

David glared at Martin. "I can drive whenever I want, Martin. There is nothing stopping me."

"That would be true if you had not surrendered your license that day. Since you no longer possess a license, nor do you have anywhere to go, perhaps you would like to work some more on your memoirs?"

"Sure, Martin. That sounds good. Where did we leave off?"

Martin turned the computer on and brought up the file. "You had just returned from the Forbidden City with the dragon piece."

David's eyes glazed over for a moment as he drifted off into the memory of days gone by. A tear made its way down his cheek, and he nodded slowly. "Yes, that was when I learned that Susan was getting married."

Chapter 19
Personal Endeavors

The first thing I did when I returned to my time was to take a shower. Agent Royceston had insisted that those tools had never been used for their advertised purpose, but I wasn't taking any chances. After a good hour of scrubbing what I hoped was mud off of my body, I flopped down onto my king-sized bed and promptly passed out.

Several hours later, I awoke to a dark house and kicked myself for not taking into account the time changes between departure and arrival. Since I had stayed awake for nearly twenty-four hours and then jumped back to my starting place and time, I had slept all day long and would now have a hard time getting back into a regular sleep pattern. Jet lag had nothing on this. Next time I would either have to set the globe to return me at bedtime or just start all my ventures into the past in the evening.

With sleep not currently an option, I decided to do some research on the next piece. I wandered into the office and booted up the computer. I brought up a search page and stared at the blinking cursor, unsure of where to start searching. The picture I had rescued from my last house was sitting on the desk next to the monitor, and I let my gaze wander over to it while I tried to collect my thoughts. On a whim, I typed in Susan's name and hit search. Apparently, our little business venture had made quite a few headlines when it had fallen apart. Poor Susan had become somewhat of a celebrity and had lost everything when the SEC seized what was left of the company. They never officially charged Susan with any wrongdoing, but they seized all of her assets along with any and all records of our investment firm. Out of desperation, and partly out of defiance, she went against the last bit of advice I had given her and joined the Army. After washing out, following my famed midnight raid on Charlie Company, she had returned home to try and get back into the market, without much luck. In the four-and-a-half years that had followed, she and her boyfriend had started up a small company offering tax services.

Another link on the search page caught my attention. It linked to a small newspaper in East Stroudsburg, and in it was a notice announcing the engagement of a James Blackwell and Susan Maryweather. I read on and found out that the wedding was to be a small gathering and would take place in three weeks in their backyard. A deep sense of loneliness spread over me, and I knew I could never hope to have a normal life as long as I pursued my mission of rescuing the genie from his bonds.

I retrieved the globe from the nightstand next to my bed, the dragon piece from the backpack, and the necklace from the safe I had recently installed in the bookshelf in the office. I placed all of the items on the desk.

"Genie, is this how all of your previous masters turned out? Paranoid and lonely? Did any of them lead a normal life?"

"Some of them tried to lead normal lives, Sir. The only one who ever came close hid me in a cave thinking she had gone mad when she heard me speak to her. Most of them became obsessed with instant gratification, limitless wealth, and power. As the old saying goes, absolute power corrupts absolutely. The more obsessed they became, the more they were distanced from society until they either went mad and killed themselves or were killed by someone else."

I rubbed my face and then asked, "So if I manage to reassemble your lamp and return you to your previous ability, I am more than likely going to succumb to the power-hungry mania that destroyed most of your previous masters? That's not a very good incentive for me to help you out, is it? I guess I could just hide you in a cave..."

The globe pulsed and I could tell that the genie wasn't keen on the idea of being hidden away after being reassembled. "You could, Sir, if that is your wish. However, you did indicate that you would release me after you had reassembled the pieces."

"So I did, didn't I. Alright, I will keep to the plan of putting you back together and setting you free, but you have to stick around afterwards to keep me out of trouble and help keep me sane."

"As you wish."

The following day I decided to take my Camaro out for the first time. Knowing that I had a bad history with that particular make and model vehicle, I had been a little nervous to even uncover it. But I figured if I could take on the Royal Guards of the Forbidden City, then I couldn't let a little car scare me. I inspected the car for more than an hour to determine if it was road worthy, and once I was satisfied, I rolled up the garage door and drove out.

I wandered without a destination in mind until I passed a bank and remembered the engagement announcement for Susan and James. An hour later, I pulled the car back into the garage and walked into the office with a cashier's check made out to the happy couple in the amount of fifty thousand dollars. I placed the check inside a simple card wishing them a long life together and signed it "from a friend." I recalled James' address from memory, addressed the envelope, and put it in the mailbox.

Several weeks passed before I found where the next piece was likely to be hidden. The genie and I had been discussing the potential whereabouts of the other pieces, but because of his inaccuracy without them, he was unable to do much more than provide a general search area. Exasperated, I flipped on the television and was surprised to find that the National Geographic Channel was running a special on the Mahabodhi Temple located in Bodh Gaya. What caught my interest was that the temple was built on the site where the Supreme Buddha, Siddhartha Gautama, supposedly found enlightenment, which coincidentally fell within the area where we had been concentrating our research.

I thought back to the story the genie had told me when I first found him. A smile came to my face as I realized the irony of how the Buddhist religion may have started. The image of Buddha was cast in the twelve hundreds A.D. in honor of Khan bringing peace to the Mongol people. It had the power to bring peace and tranquility to anyone within its sphere of influence. It had been taken back to the sixth century B.C. and given to the man credited with the creation of the Buddhist "Middle Way," on perhaps the very spot where he is said to have found enlightenment.

As I continued to watch the special on the Mahabodhi Temple, I started to formulate a plan for getting into the temple and searching for the Buddha piece. I knew I couldn't go back to when it was given to the Siddhartha Gautama. The genie and I felt certain that the powers of the piece had some influence on Siddhartha and all of his followers. The narrator mentioned that the temple was rebuilt by the British in 1880, and I knew at once where, and more importantly when, I had to go. I would travel back to when the British were restoring the temple. With all the workers and architects crawling all over the site, it would be easy to conduct a search. All I would have to do is look for a group of workers who appeared more at peace than any other, and the piece should be fairly close-by. However, if my previous expeditions into the past were any indication of things to come, this trip would be far from easy. I slipped into a set of khaki-colored fatigues and put on a safari hat to complete the look. After concealing my knife under the back of my shirt with the hilt facing down, I grabbed the backpack, put the necklace along with all of my essentials in it, and spun the dial on the globe.

Chapter 20
Buddha Search

With a flash I appeared. I had jumped back to 1:30 A.M. on the 13th of April, 1883, into what I hoped was an empty field. It was pitch black, and I waited for a moment for my eyes to adjust to the darkness. It slowly dawned on me that I wasn't standing in the middle of an empty field. I reached into my bag and pulled out my flashlight. Carefully, I covered the lens with my hand and turned it on. What I was able to see with the little bit of light I let out between my fingers made my heart sink into my boots. I had managed to land in the middle of what appeared to be the tent of a British government official. Judging by the accoutrements in the tent, this individual was fairly important. After a quick glance around the interior, I found the sole occupant sleeping soundly on a large cot surrounded by a mosquito net. A flash of reflected light caught my attention. Hanging on a peg next to the cot was an intricately made British officer's sword, with the initials "A.C." delicately engraved on the scabbard.

I quietly made my way outside and had made it no more than a couple yards from the tent when I heard the distinct sound of a revolver hammer being pulled back and the gravelly voice of a British captain.

"Just stay where you are, there's a good lad. Now, why don't you tell me what you're doing poking around my camp?"

I quickly slipped my flashlight into my pocket and turned around. The captain was easily six feet tall and impressively broad in the shoulders. His no-nonsense demeanor put across the image that he was used to his orders being obeyed the first time, yet there was something vaguely familiar about him.

I tried to think of a plausible excuse, "Sir, I am an American reporter sent to investigate the rebuilding of the Mahabodhi Temple. I have been walking since early this morning trying to find the site without much luck. I had about given up when I stumbled upon your camp here. Judging by the uniform, you're a captain, right? Are you involved with the reconstruction? Do you know Director-General Cunningham? Can you direct–"

The captain cut me off with a wave of his hand.

"Slow down, lad. Let's see now... Yes, I am a captain. Captain Royceston. And yes, you could say that I'm involved with the reconstruction project. I am in charge of security around here. As for knowing the director-general, you just walked past his tent over there. Now it's my turn to ask the questions. You said you have been walking all day, where from?"

I thought back to the documentary on the National Geographic Channel that I had watched. "My guide left me about thirty miles down the Phalgu River and told me to follow it south and I would find my way."

Captain Royceston holstered his pistol and scratched his head. "Why would your guide abandon you like that? Did you say or do something to offend him?"

"I don't think so... We had stopped at a small roadside cafe to grab a bite to eat and halfway through lunch he said he could no longer abide my insensitivity, told me which direction to travel, and then promptly left."

The captain thought for a moment and then said, "Tell me exactly what happened during your meal."

"Well, when we first arrived, my guide asked me what I would like to eat. I told him that I could kill for a good steak and he gave me the strangest look. Then I opened the door to the dusty-looking establishment and held it open for him. He still looked a little put out about the steak comment so I gave him a little push through the door. Once we–"

"Which hand did you use to push him through the door?"

I thought for a moment before answering, "Left, I think..."

"Right. Go on then."

"Um, let's see, ah yes, once we were inside and had gotten our food–"

"What did you have to eat?"

"We had some kind of rice dish served on top of a big leaf. It looked all right, but it smelled ghastly. There were other dishes that I thought were for us to share, however every time I would help myself to some of the various foods, my guide would look disgusted with me, and he finally got up and left."

Captain Royceston began to chuckle. "Bloody Yank. You're lucky that bloke didn't try to kill you. You insulted his religion by asking for a steak and you violated his personal space by touching him, with your left hand no less. If I were a betting man, I would say that you were taking food from the community bowls with the same hand that you were eating with weren't you?"

I hung my head in what I was hoping was a convincing show of shame. The captain continued with a grin on his face.

"Cheer up, lad. You're here now. But I'm afraid the director-general doesn't like to be bothered at night so you will have to wait until morning, and since it's not safe to go out after dark, I suggest we find you a place to bed down for the night."

I smiled, "That would be very nice, Sir."

The smell of coffee and the sounds of the campsite woke

me several hours later. The captain had been kind enough to lend me a spare cot which, judging by the way my neck and back felt when I awoke, may or may not have been better than sleeping on the ground. I quickly went through my backpack to make sure nobody had taken anything during the night, then set out to find breakfast.

I hadn't made it very far before Captain Royceston appeared at my side. His ability to sneak up on me was very unnerving and yet somehow familiar. "The Director-General would like to have you join him for breakfast. If you would follow me..."

I didn't think I had a choice, and since I was hungry anyway, I decided to follow him. As he led me in silence back to the director-general's tent, I took the opportunity to get a good look at the camp. From what I could see, the general's tent was just off a parade field located in the center of the camp with rows upon rows of tents in every direction. It took me a moment to find the temple ruins in the distance and by the time I did, Captain Royceston was impatiently directing me into the director-general's tent. I couldn't read the expression on his face, yet for some reason he didn't look happy. He didn't say anything as I entered the tent, nor did he stay long. He merely introduced me to Sir Alexander Cunningham, then let himself out of the tent, closing the entrance flap as he did so.

General Cunningham was an older gentleman dressed not in the traditional military uniform, but in a dark-colored three-piece suit. The chain of a pocket watch could just be seen peeking out from under the right side of his jacket and hooked into the second buttonhole of his vest. His large, white, bushy mustache and thick goatee obscured most of his facial expression, yet his eyes were intense, and I had the feeling he wouldn't believe the story I had told the captain. I could feel sweat start to bead up on my forehead, and I started to fidget as he continued to pick me apart with his gaze. He was seated on a small wooden chair that appeared to be straining under the load, and on the table next to him was a large breakfast with service for two. After what seemed like hours, he invited me to sit across from him at the table with a wave of his hand. When he finally spoke, it was with a calm but authoritative voice.

"Captain Royceston tells me you are an American reporter." He picked up a biscuit, broke it in half, and dipped half of it in some honey that was on the plate in front of him. "He also told me that you wandered into camp in the middle of the night after having walked all day because you insulted your guide to the point that he abandoned you somewhere down the Phalgu River." He took a bite of his biscuit and then continued, "Frankly, I don't believe it and neither does the captain."

I sat for a moment stunned. The general continued to scrutinize me over the table as he ate his breakfast. I picked up a glass of water that was next to my plate and took a swallow in an attempt to replace the moisture that had suddenly left my mouth.

"What don't you believe?" I hoped my voice didn't squeak as much as it sounded to me like it did.

"I don't believe any of it. First off, it was incredibly hot yesterday, and you don't look like someone who walked all day in the sun. Your clothes are too clean and your skin isn't burnt. Speaking of your clothes, they look more like a military uniform than those of a reporter. The good captain said he was out using the loo last night when he saw a bright flash of light coming from the inside of my tent. When he went to investigate, he found you wandering not too far from here. He said you looked nervous and started asking a myriad of questions. After getting you a place to sleep, he posted two guards to watch you and then came to check on me."

He paused in his speech to take another bite of biscuit and honey. He wiped the crumbs off of his mustache before he started to speak again. "He told me your story, he told me his side of the story, and then he told me what he believed you were really doing here."

"And what is it that he believes I am doing here, Sir?" I knew that whatever he believed, I could deny, unless of course...

"He believes you are here to steal some of the relics from the archeological dig at the Mahabodhi Temple in order to sell them to wealthy collectors, like the tomb raiders in Egypt. However, after a short investigation, I believe you are not after some generic relics; rather, you are looking for something specific. And judging by the tracks on the floor of my tent and the fact that nothing of mine is missing, you believe that whatever it is you are looking for is still in the temple."

I glanced down at my untouched breakfast and wondered what I was going to tell him. He had most of my story figured out, minus the time traveling bit and the real reason as to why I was in his tent of course, so it probably wouldn't hurt to expound upon what he perceived to be the truth.

"It is true that what I seek is not in this tent. Nor is it in this campsite. It is one of two missing pieces to a collection produced by a blacksmith for none other than Genghis Khan. These pieces are said to have mystical powers, and each one affects people in a different way. For example," I reached into my bag and pulled out the dragon piece, "This piece was made in honor of Khan's military might and it gives the possessor absolute authority."

"Poppycock! That little trinket can no more give someone power than I can fly like a bird. Preposterous."

I could see that he would need a demonstration, so I decided to try something. I used my most authoritative voice and gave a single command.

"Bark like a dog."

The director-general sat up straight in his chair, his eyes seemed to glass over, and with the oddest look on his face he replied, "I don't see any reason why I shouldn't." At that, he proceeded to bark like a Boston Terrier greeting the mailman. It really was an impressive dog impersonation. If I closed my eyes, I could clearly imagine a small ball of fur with razor-sharp teeth trying to break through a screen door in an attempt to gnaw the leg off an unsuspecting postal carrier. It seemed a shame to bring it to an end.

"That's enough, Sir." The director-general stopped barking. I put the dragon piece back into my bag. When I looked back up, his eyes had cleared and he did not look amused.

"I believe you. I don't know how it works, but I believe you. What else do you have in that odd-looking bag of tricks, boy? Why don't you just hand it over so I can take a look."

When I refused to hand over my bag, he reached behind himself and retrieved his sword which was still hanging next to his cot. He stood up, wielding it in his right hand and slowly advanced toward me.

I looked around to find a way to escape, but he was between me and the only exit. I adopted my voice of authority again and told him to drop his sword and sit down. The point of his sword dipped about three quarters of an inch, and he stopped his advance. A smile spread slowly across his face and he brought the point back up.

"How interesting. It appears that you need to have the dragon in your hand in order to impose your will on others. Now, drop the bag, boy."

He punctuated his demand by lunging forward and taking a swipe with his sword. The blade just barely missed my knuckles as I retreated around the table. I reached behind

my back and drew out my survival knife and held it up in
what I hoped was a defensive manner. When I had purchased
that particular knife it had seemed huge. The twelve-inch
blade was impressive looking in the showcase, but compared
to the thirty-six-inch-long blade of the sword before me, it
left much to be desired.

The director-general smiled and shook his head. He
was about to make some sort of comment, but he never got
the chance. When he opened his mouth to speak, I flipped
the knife, caught it by the blade, and launched it as hard as
I could directly at his head. The hilt of the knife struck him
between the eyes with a loud *thunk*. His eyes crossed briefly,
and he went down like a felled tree.

I ran around the table and knelt beside him to check
his pulse and was relieved when I found one. I dug through
my bag until I found the roll of duct tape. Quickly I taped
his hands together behind his back and then bound his feet
together. I placed a large strip over his mouth and retrieved
my knife.

I was surprised that our fight hadn't drawn any interest,
but I knew it was only a matter of time before someone came
to check on the director-general and the word got out. I had
to find the Buddha piece and get home as soon as possible.
I peeked out the tent flap, and my heart sank into my boots.
Twenty or so soldiers stood in a semi-circle taking orders
from the captain who was pointing emphatically at the
director-general's tent.

I ran to the far side of the tent, cut a hole through
the wall, and started digging through my bag. I pulled
out the necklace and put it on. I waited for some sort of
transformation, but I felt nothing. I pulled out the globe and
voiced my concern.

"I thought I was supposed to become irresistibly
attractive when I put this on. I don't feel any different, nor do

I look any different. What's going on here?"

The globe buzzed for a second before the genie answered, "Sir, beauty is in the eye of the beholder. The fact that you have not seen any difference is a kind of safety feature. You will not see any difference directly, but, be forewarned, if you see yourself in a mirror or any other reflective surface, you may wind up like poor Narcissus."

"I don't believe I have any predilection toward homosexuality. I don't care how attractive this thing makes me look, I won't wind up like that Greek myth."

"Sir, I do not believe –"

The genie didn't get the chance to finish that statement. Three soldiers burst into the tent and swept the room with their rifles. When they saw me, they stopped and stared with their mouths agape. One of them let out a low whistle and pushed one of the others back out of the tent. Once he was outside, I heard the captain demand a report. The soldier's response was a little muffled, but I was still able to make it out.

"The tent is secure, Sir. The director-general is tied up and appears to be unconscious, but there is no sign of the young man you described. There is however–"

The captain cut off the report, the anger in his voice evident even inside the tent. "What do you mean there is no sign of him?! He has to be in there somewhere."

Pushing his way past the reporting soldier, he charged into the tent and looked around. He seemed a little dazed when he saw me, but he quickly regained his composure and got down to business.

"I don't know who you are or how you got in here, nor do I care. All I want to know is which way the American went, then you can go about your business." His voice softened and he put his hands on my shoulders. "You're not in trouble, I know you didn't do this to the director-general.

Just tell me which way the young man who was just in here went." I nervously pointed to the slash I had cut through the side of the tent and the captain and his men rushed out.

When I was sure the search party was gone, I slipped out the front of the tent and quickly made my way across the camp toward the temple in the distance. I had only gone a short way when I started to notice the same slack-jawed stares I had received in the tent. The conversation of two soldiers caught my attention.

"Hey, would you get a look at that! We don't get many of those out here!"

"You leave that boy alone, he ain't hurting nobody."

"Boy?!? I think you need..."

Their voices faded as I continued on my way. Soon I was at the edge of the camp, which sat right on the bank of the river. As I stood there trying to figure out how to cross the half-mile-wide, swift-moving river, I noticed a large group of soldiers coming toward me.

The soldier in front of the pack leered at me and called over his shoulder, "Alright, boys, it's time to have some fun."

Faced with a mob of soldiers bent on mischief, I did what anyone in my position would do–I ran for my life. I ran along the beach for a short distance and then turned back into the camp, hoping to lose them in the tents. After making several turns, I spotted an open tent flap. I dove in and pulled it shut behind me. About thirty seconds later, the mob thundered passed, and I let out a sigh of relief. Some movement caught my eye at the other end of the tent. I sat very still until my eyes adjusted to the dim lighting. At the other end of the tent sat a very scared and familiar-looking young lady.

After a moment or two, the memory of when I had last seen this young woman hit me, and my blood ran cold. I could almost hear the air-raid sirens and smell the smoke from the fires set by the German bombers. The image of her broken body in the rubble just before I removed the necklace I was now wearing would be one that I would never forget. I shook my head and tried to force the image of the curator of the Lady Godiva Museum from my mind. The young lady at the other end of the tent also shook her head, and another thought crossed my mind. Hoping I was wrong, I stood up and started walking toward my female companion, who also stood up and started walking toward me. My suspicions were confirmed when I reached the mirror in the center of the tent. Slowly I removed the necklace from around my neck and watched my reflection melt back into what I really looked like.

"This is what you were trying to warn me about, wasn't it Genie? I don't feel any kind of attraction toward my reflection, though. So much for your Narcissus theory." I pulled the globe out of my pocket as it began to buzz.

"Yes, Sir. The fact that you had seen someone use the necklace may have prepared you in some way for who, or what, you saw. The person you perceived yourself to be is the same image you would see regardless of who was wearing the necklace."

I put the necklace back on and watched my reflection change once again. As I looked at the image in the mirror, a thought occurred to me. "Genie, how does the necklace work? Have I seen this person before, or is it my subconscious manifestation of the perfect woman?"

"It is possible, Sir, that you have seen someone very similar to what you see, as the necklace works with your mind and picks the most attractive traits from your memories. However, even if you knew someone you thought was perfect, there would always be minor differences, whether it is clearer skin, longer or shorter hair, or even just the color of the eyes."

"Minor differences..." I studied the vision before me with shoulder-length blonde hair and delicate facial features. I knew I had seen this person before, but for some reason I couldn't remember where. As I studied the eyes, it dawned on me, there was only one person I knew who had eyes that shade of blue, and she would never want to speak to me again. Not after what I did to her when I dissolved our company.

I removed the necklace, and as I was placing it back into my backpack, the genie gave me some advice.

"Sir, I would suggest that you continue to wear the necklace. Without it, the guards will recognize you and attempt to capture you. You are still wanted for assault on the director-general."

"Genie, I appreciate the concern. However, I believe I would prefer to be captured and delivered to Captain Royceston rather than face what that last group had on its mind."

"I see your point, Sir."

I stuck my head out of the tent and when I was sure it was safe, I made my way back to where the mob started chasing me. Off in the distance, I could just make out the top of the temple. Just up the river, tied to a small makeshift dock, were a couple of longboats. I ran over to one of them and dove in. The first thing I noticed was that the oars were missing. After a quick search, I discovered a thick rope anchored to the end of the dock, tightly stretched across the river. A pair of small ropes were attached to the thicker rope with metal rings, with one tied to the bow and the other tied to the stern.

I untied the dock line from the boat and grabbed onto the thick rope spanning the river. Slowly, I pulled myself and the boat across the river.

Chapter 21
Buddha Retrieval

Crossing the river was exhausting. To make matters worse, someone had seen me and sounded the alarm. Thirty yards behind me and gaining was the second boat, loaded down with British troops. Standing on the bow was none other than Captain Royceston himself. By the time I reached the far side of the river, the other boat had reduced my lead by half, and I knew I didn't have enough energy left to outrun the twenty or so troops who were on board.

As soon as I was close enough to the dock, I jumped onto it, pulled out my knife, and started sawing my way through the thick rope they were using to pull themselves along. Several of the troops saw what I was attempting to do and opened fire with their rifles, only to be stopped by the captain. I heard him admonishing them and explaining that the director-general wanted me alive.

Just as the boat came within a few feet of the dock, I was able to cut through the main rope. Since the rope was pulled tight, it snapped back with considerable force, causing everyone who was holding onto the rope to fall backwards. One unlucky soul had his hand pulled through one of the rings that tied the boat to the mainline, making it impossible to free the boat from the large rope. The boat drifted downstream, and since the mainline was still tied to the west dock, it pulled the boat back across to the west side of the river. Captain Royceston and several of his soldiers dove overboard in an attempt to swim to the eastern bank. The swift current pushed them several hundred yards downstream before they were able to pull themselves from the water.

As I made my way into the ruins, I pulled out the globe.

"Genie, if there is any way you can help me find the Buddha piece, I would greatly appreciate it."

The globe pulsed lightly and the genie's voice answered, "I cannot give you any specific directions, however, I can tell you that we are getting much closer. It is nearby. I suggest you observe the workers in the area. Most will be in a foul mood working in this hot environment under military supervision. However, any person or persons within the sphere of influence of the piece will show signs of euphoria and be at peace with their situation."

"Look for happy people. Right. All I need is a group of people to walk around to use as canaries." I slipped the globe back into my pocket and started my search. Twenty or so minutes later, I hadn't come any closer to finding the Buddha when I felt the muzzle of the captain's revolver being pressed in between my shoulder blades.

"That was quite a little stunt you pulled back there, lad. Now you will come back with me quietly, or I will carry you back, and let the doc patch you back up."

I raised my hands and slowly turned around. I thought about making a grab for his pistol, but I quickly put those thoughts aside when I saw the eight soldiers behind him with their rifles at the ready. I felt the globe pulse in my pocket and I heard the genie say, "Sir, here are your canaries."

I smiled at the comment which made everyone uneasy, since I was the only one who could hear the genie. The captain tightened his grip on his pistol and took a step back. I shook my head and tried to put him at ease.

"Captain, do you know why the director-general wants me?" When he didn't answer I continued, "I have discovered a set of items of incalculable value, and he wants to take them away from me. I explained to him that I believed there was another item from this set hidden among the ruins here and that it was my mission to bring all these items back together.

Let me show you the one I showed the director-general."

I very slowly removed my backpack and reached inside. Everyone tensed, expecting trouble. One of the soldiers fired his rifle, and I heard the bullet snap past my ear. I grabbed the dragon, felt the confidence surge through me, and yelled for everyone to lower their weapons and stand at attention. For a moment nobody moved. Then, one by one, they all pointed their muzzles toward the ground and stood up straight. Captain Royceston was the last one to comply, but after a long, tense moment, he holstered his pistol.

I looked around at the soldiers before me. They were all confused and more than a little angry. All except the captain. There was no confusion in his eyes, just pure anger.

When he found his voice, I knew I wouldn't be able to put the dragon piece down until I was ready to depart, "The director warned me of your mystical golden trinkets. Frankly, I didn't believe his ranting, but I see that he was telling the truth. You will release me from this spell–"

I cut him off with a wave of my hand. "All in good time, Captain. All in good time. Right now I need your help. I want all of your men to walk ahead of me, two by two, three meters apart. We are going to search until we find it. Captain, you will stay by my side and make no attempt to overpower me or escape. Let's go."

His men glared at me, but did as I ordered. The captain himself seemed to fight against the power of the dragon piece but eventually took his place at my side. With everyone in place, I ordered the line of soldiers to proceed into the temple. An hour or so later, we emerged from the temple next to a large tree. I had the men turn left and follow the wall. The wall had intricately-carved Buddhas all along it. After inspecting the wall, I had the men turn toward the tree itself. The tree had a small temple underneath it, and I asked the captain what the significance of the tree was. He explained that this was the Mahabodhi Tree under which Siddhartha Gautama attained enlightenment. He went on to give me a history lesson on the temple.

As we approached the tree, I noticed the men in front of the line start to relax. After a few more steps, the next two in line visibly relaxed as well. The closer we came to the tree, the more the men seemed to be at peace. When I came within thirty or so feet of the tree, I felt the effects wash over me like a warm wave. All the tension in my body seemed to melt away, and I felt as though everything was going to be alright. Even the captain seemed to be happy, and the barest hint of a smile could be seen on his lips.

I ordered everyone to stop and stand at ease. They all did as I ordered and even smiled at me as I made my way into the small temple by the tree. Inside I found not one, but a wall of small golden Buddha statues. Had it not been for the effects of the piece I was looking for, I would probably have screamed in frustration. An idea came to mind, and I stuck my head back out the door.

"Captain, would you go stand back over there a ways?"

The captain just nodded and happily complied. At least he was happy until he moved out of range of the Buddha piece. Almost instantly his face screwed up into a fierce scowl, and he appeared to be fighting once again against my orders. When I felt he had gone far enough, I ordered him to stop and turn around. He spun and glared at me.

"OK, that's good."

I ducked back inside and grabbed one of the statues. Holding it before me, I walked out of the temple toward the captain. When his demeanor didn't change, I knew I had the wrong one. I ran back, replaced it, and picked up another. One by one I brought out the statues until I saw the captain relax. I walked back and forth with the Buddha watching his face change from anger to contentment and back until I was convinced that I had the correct one.

I ordered all of his men to return to the camp and get on with their regular duties. When they had all gone, I turned to the captain and smiled. "Captain Benjamin Royceston, it has been a pleasure working with you. Do me a favor and say 'Hi' to your son James for me, would you?"

I pulled out the globe and had myself transported back to my own place and time, leaving the bewildered captain an unbelievable story to tell his future son.

Chapter 22
Present Day

Martin stopped typing and turned at the sound of David coughing. The coughing and wheezing had been getting gradually worse over the past few days, and today was the worst yet. Martin's concern grew when he saw David's ashen complexion. When he couldn't get any response out of his boss, he quickly loaded him into the car and drove him to the hospital.

At the hospital, Martin waited anxiously for any word on his friend's condition. After a couple hours, the doctor came out to the waiting room and delivered the news.

"Mr. Smith, we've moved David out of the ICU and into a private room. We have him stabilized for the moment, but I'm afraid his condition is deteriorating rapidly. It's only a matter of time now. I'm sorry."

Martin nodded his head. "May I go and see him?"

The doctor pointed down the hall, "Go down that hall and take the first left. His is the third door on the right. Do not let him take off his mask. It's the only thing keeping him stable at the moment."

Martin nodded again and set off down the hall. When he entered David's room, he wasn't surprised to find him feebly trying to remove the oxygen mask covering his face. He gently placed his hand on his friend's shoulder and David stopped pulling at his mask.

"Martin," David's voice could just barely be heard over the machines in the room.

Martin leaned in closer, "Yes, Sir?"

David sat with his eyes closed for a minute before continuing, "I want you to go home and get the laptop. We need to finish my memoirs soon. I don't know how much longer I have–"

A coughing fit racked David's body causing him to convulse pitifully on his bed. By the time the fit subsided, several new alarms had started to go off on one of the various machines he was hooked up to. As David slowly recovered, the alarms turned off one by one until once again all that was left was the soft beeps and whirs of the monitors.

Martin pulled up a chair next to the bed and picked up a pad of paper and a pen that a nurse had thoughtfully left in the room. "Sir, if it is alright with you, I will hand write the rest while I am here and type it up later."

"That will...be fine...Martin."

Three hours later, Martin had all the details he needed to write out the end of his good friend's memoirs, except for one minor point.

"Sir, I do not believe we ever covered what happened to Private Jameson. I know it is a minor point, however, we did leave that part of your life story unresolved. How would you like me to address that situation?"

Martin looked up from his notes and noticed that David had become unresponsive. His breathing had been becoming increasingly labored, and his speech had been slow and slurred during the last hour of the interview. A new alarm started to chime on one of the machines in the room, and a nurse hurried in. She read the display and made some notations on David's chart before asking Martin to join her in the hallway. Martin set down his pad of paper and followed her out, already knowing what was to come.

"Mr. Smith, it's only a matter of minutes. He has put up an incredible fight against this disease, but his lung function has dropped to the point that he will never regain consciousness. We could keep his body alive on respirators and oxygen, but we both know he wouldn't want that." Her voice softened and she took one of Martin's hands in hers before continuing. "Sometimes all they need is a friend or loved one to tell them everything is taken care of and it's OK for them to let go now."

Martin placed his other hand on the nurse's shoulder and thanked her for all she had done for his friend and returned to the room. He quietly walked over to David's bed and took his hand. "The nurse just told me that it will not be long now. I do not believe she knows just how stubborn you can be. However, I want you to know that I will finish out your memoirs, as per your request, and everything will be taken care of. Now, my friend it is time for you rest, it is time for you to go home."

He gave David's hand one last squeeze and turned to gather up his papers. David took one last breath, his body seemed to shudder a little as he exhaled, then he lay completely still. The monitor above his bed let out a solid tone and Martin reached up and silenced it with the push of a button. He gathered his belongings and stepped out into the hall. Once again he thanked the nurse for all she had done, then left.

Chapter 23
From Martin's Notes

Martin booted up the office computer, pulled out his notes and began to organize his thoughts. He tried to imagine the way David would have told how he retrieved the last piece. He read over his notes one last time, then started typing.

After a few days of recuperation, I decided there was no time like the present to explore the past for a future possession.

Martin chuckled to himself as he reread what he had just typed. "I bet if David were here he would say, 'that was a tense opening statement.' " He sobered up, sighed, and quietly got back to work.

When several hours had past, I was still no closer to discovering where the ring might be located. I pulled out the globe and consulted the genie on where he had last seen the ring.

"Sir, as I told you before, the last time I saw the ring was as it was buried underneath the base of an incredibly large tower that was being built in the land of Shinar."

"OK, I remember you telling me that much... Shinar... That name sounds familiar. Where have I heard that before?" Before the genie could answer, I reached for the only book in my library that didn't have a thick layer of dust on it, my Bible. In the book of Genesis, chapter eleven, verse two, *"And it came to pass, as they journeyed from the east, that they found a plain in the land of Shinar; and they dwelt there."*

As I read on, the pieces started to finally click into place, but I had to be sure.

"Genie, is this the tower that is referenced in the book of Genesis?"

"That is correct, Sir."

"Then explain to me why you described the location of the ring as 'buried underneath the base of an incredibly large tower that was being built in the land of Shinar.' Why didn't you just call it by its name?"

"As you have surmised, it is in fact, the Tower of Babel where the Lord confounded the language of all men and scattered them abroad upon the face of the earth. Khan's servant was present during the Great Confusion, although the tower was struck after he hid the ring. As for my choice of description, it was not called Babel when the servant and I arrived."

"Alright, Genie, where was this tower in the land of Shinar? And is there anything built over the top of the site today? I don't exactly want to end up like Khan's servant, if you know what I mean."

"Sir, I believe if you bring all the pieces we have collected together, I may be able to show you the spot to which the servant jumped. Give or take a few hundred feet. However, in this instance, it would be beneficial if you went back to the time it was hidden to retrieve it."

"Genie, I do not want to risk getting caught in the Great Confusion if at all possible. Let's explore the ruins first."

I quickly brought all the pieces together as instructed and waited. The globe pulsed for a moment or two before the genie continued, "The site where it was hidden is located in what has become northeastern Syria, not far from the city of Tell Brak. If you will direct your attention to that area on the globe..." A small green dot appeared in the area the genie had described. "And no, there is nothing built on top of the ruins.

However, time has buried the site and worn away all traces of the foundations."

I started to put together a list of the things I would have to bring. For starters, I would have to have a good shovel, and possibly a pick, to excavate the ruins. It probably wouldn't hurt to have a metal detector as well.

After gathering all my supplies and changing into a set of khaki-colored fatigues and boots, I picked up the globe and placed my finger on the green dot. I took one last look around and had the genie transport me to the location of the ruins.

Chapter 24
So Close...

    I appeared in a clearing at the base of an enormous hill. There was little vegetation anywhere around and absolutely no sign of civilization, past or present. There didn't seem to be any ruins at all. The only thing out of place was the massive hill I was standing before, as the rest of the land I could see was flat, with the exception of the mountains in the distance to the east. I walked around the base of the hill looking for some indication that I was in the right area. After three or four hours, I was only a third of the way around the hill when I found a perfectly rectangular rock about four feet long on one side and one foot square on the ends. The most interesting thing about the rock was not its size or shape, but the strange markings carved down the length of one of the sides.

ΗΕΡΕϚΛΑΝΓΥΑΓΕϚΑϚΤΗΡΟΥΓΗϚΠΕΟΠΛΕ ϚΥΝΙΤΕΔϚΤΗΑΤϚΟΦϚΚΙΝΓϚΡΙΝΓϚΛΙΕΣ

    I sat down next to the block and pulled out the globe.
    "Genie, since you have the ability to change the language displayed on the globe, do you think you could help me identify and possibly translate these markings?"
    The globe vibrated for a moment before answering, "I have seen these markings before, and though it was a written and spoken language, there was only one person to ever use it. These markings were left by the servant of Khan on the lintel of the tunnel's entrance as a clue to what he had hidden deep under the tower."
    Excitement ran through me like a bolt of lightning.

"So we're close, very close." I looked over at the large mound that must have been the remains of the tower and my shoulders sagged. "Yet so far away..."

I didn't think my lone shovel and pick were going to make a dent in that pile in my lifetime. I had to come up with a different plan to retrieve the ring, and even though I had told the genie that I wanted to avoid going back to the tower before it was destroyed, it looked like my only option. I flipped over the globe and thought for a moment before asking the genie for one more piece of information.

"Genie, I believe you were right, and we are going to have to go back in time in order to have a chance at finding the ring. What I need to know is when was the tower destroyed and the languages confounded?"

I waited in silence for a few minutes and started to think that the genie wasn't going to answer me when the globe pulsed very lightly and spoke. "Bear in mind that this jaunt into the past will be very dangerous. The people of that time had turned themselves away from God to the point of defiance. You will have to be on your guard the entire time and spend as little time as possible there. And above all else, you have to be out of there before the Lord comes down to confound the languages. To answer your question, the year was 2242 B.C. The month was October, and the day was Friday, the 24th."

I spun the rings on the bottom of the globe and thought of one more question, "Will a jump this far into the past affect me worse than the others?"

The genie seemed to be laughing as it responded, "You may want to go backward an extra day to give yourself time to recover. This jump will be unlike any you have attempted thus far."

I made the adjustment to the target date, closed my eyes, and made the jump.

Chapter 25
The Tower

The genie wasn't exaggerating when he told me I would need time to recover. The world seemed to spin and swirl around me like so many oil paints in a centrifuge. After what seemed like hours, my vision started to clear, and I found myself staring up the side of an enormous structure which looked like a stepped pyramid and seemed to disappear into the heavens above. I had set the target time to one in the morning, hoping my arrival would go unnoticed. Apparently, I was wrong to think that the people of ancient times wouldn't work at night because of the lack of light.

All around the base and on every level up the tower as far as the eye could see were torches. Thousands of workers streamed to the construction site from a nearby city carrying supplies and tools. The tower itself was crawling with hundreds more, all of whom were laying brick, carving stone, or hoisting supplies up with massive cranes made of wood and rope. Even the children were hard at work, carrying what appeared to be food and water to the workers.

When a few more moments had passed, I began to take stock of my immediate surroundings. I was lying on the ground propped up against a wall that seemed to stretch for miles in either direction. To my right was a gate through the wall, at my back and to my left was what appeared to be a forge for making brick and other pottery.

My appearance had not gone unnoticed, as I had hoped. Half a dozen or so people lay before me as if worshiping an idol. Before I could do or say anything, I felt the globe vibrate in my hand and the voice of the genie cut through the fog that was still thick between my ears. The panic in the genie's voice made the hair on the back of my neck stand on end.

"Sir, I highly suggest you do not speak at all. If you remember your Sunday School lessons correctly, you will realize that these people would have never heard any other language than their own. Furthermore, you should consider placing the globe into your backpack, lest one of these people take it from you."

Slowly, I picked up my backpack and placed the globe in the main pocket and took a quick inventory: one canteen of water, the Taser, two cans of pepper spray, the laser pointer, a powerful flashlight, duct tape, the necklace, Buddha, dragon, and of course, the globe.

I checked my watch, which I had set to one o'clock just before making the jump, and was astonished to find that the time was almost four thirty. My small group of worshipers noticed I was awake and moving around, and they started to shout. One of them jumped to his feet and ran the fifty or so yards to the base of the tower where a large group of men in ornate robes was standing. When he had their attention, they started toward me in what looked like a very ceremonial manner.

Thinking about what the genie had said about speaking to these people, I began to search for an avenue of escape. I stood up straight with my feet planted shoulder width apart. I slung the backpack onto my back and cinched the straps tight. Slowly, I raised my outstretched arms and began to hum a low and continuous note. As I lifted my arms, I increased the volume of my voice. All the people still prostrate at my feet began to take on a fearful look and back away.

The oncoming procession, which I assumed to be the high priest and his entourage, slowed and came to a halt when they saw their people beginning to panic. When I was certain I had their attention, I clapped my hands together, pointing at the top of the tower before me and let out a scream. Everyone in attendance immediately snapped around to look at the top of the tower. With the crowd looking the other way, I sprinted the twenty feet to my right toward the gate and dove through it.

The city itself looked as if it could have been from modern day. The main street through the center of town ran east and west and was approximately fifty feet wide. It was lined with shops on either side, all of which were closed except for what appeared to be a bakery on the south side of the street. The smells of a wood-fired oven and fresh-baked breads drifted heavily through the air. Behind the shops were row upon row of houses laid out in a perfectly square grid pattern. Each house was two stories tall and faced toward the east, looking toward the outside wall and the massive tower. On each side of the houses were streets half as wide as the main street. The buildings and the streets looked as if they were made of a reddish-colored concrete which I assumed was hard packed clay. In the center of each of the north- and south-running side streets were tiles roughly twenty-four inches wide and thirty-six inches long. On the west wall of each dwelling was a column of matching tiles leading down to a row of tiles in the street that connected to the row in the center of the street.

As soon as I came in through the gate, it was apparent that I wouldn't be able to disappear in the crowd as I had hoped. It wasn't for the lack of people, there were people everywhere, more so than I would have thought that early in the morning, it was because I looked so different from everyone else. All the people I could see were wearing some sort of off-white material draped over themselves like a poncho and tied around the waist like a robe. Their skin color was nut brown, where mine was as light as their clothing. If it had been dark, as I had hoped, I could have hidden myself in the shadows. However, just like around the base of the tower, the streets were all alight with torch light.

Standing in the center of the street, I quickly drew the attention of everyone around me. For a few seconds I stood still, unsure of what I should do next. I was forced into action when a large group of people entered the city led by a man I believed was the head priest. The priest raised his hand, pointed at me, and gave a simple command. The mob behind him surged forward, anger and hatred in their eyes. Deciding it was time to go, I took off at a dead sprint. Not west down the main street, but north along the outer wall, with the angry mob close behind. I followed the outer wall for a short distance and then ducked down a side street. In an attempt to lose the mob, I took the next left I came to and looked for some place to hide. There on the back side of that building where the tiles from the street met the tiles on the wall was the best place I could see.

The tiles on the backs of the buildings covered what appeared to be a shallow channel roughly eight inches deep and twenty inches wide. On this particular building, the tiles had fallen off, exposing the perfect hiding spot. The inside of the channel was slick with what appeared to be some kind of foul-smelling mold, but at that moment, as long as it concealed me I didn't care. I stuffed my bag down into the bottom and just managed to wedge myself in when the mob rounded the corner looking for me.

The mob consisted of eighty or so people and quickly passed me by. Just to be safe, I stayed in my hiding spot for perhaps ten minutes, until I heard voices inside the house I was hiding behind. I couldn't understand their language, but it sounded like they were getting closer, and I started to panic. An odd scraping noise startled me, and I looked up the crevice I was hiding in just in time to get a face full of what could only be urine and fecal matter. I had been hiding in the drainage pipe for the indoor toilets!

I was so startled by the foul shower that I let out a scream which, of course, let the people who were looking for me know exactly where I was. It didn't take them long to find me, and I soon found myself, once again, running for my life. This time I ran back to the south toward the main road, and by the time I got there, the mob behind me had grown to over a hundred people. Once I crossed the main road I found myself behind the bakery I had seen earlier. I ducked in through the back door and was immediately confronted by a rather portly and stern looking man who could only be the baker. He didn't seem too happy that I had just invaded his establishment covered in filth.

We eyed each other for a moment before the sound of my pursuers began to echo through the shop. I couldn't understand what they were yelling, but something they said seemed to spook the baker, and he grabbed a wooden dowel that looked like it could be either a rolling pin or a billy club. Feeling like I had overstayed my welcome, I turned to run back out the door, only to find it blocked by a couple of large individuals. The only other avenue of escape was a small staircase that led up to the second floor. I bolted up the stairs and through a heavy curtain at the top expecting to find a small apartment or possibly an office. Instead, I emerged into a room with no ceiling where the baker kept his chickens and goats.

The walls of the room were just over eight feet tall and looked as if there had been a roof at one point. Holes about the size of a man's fist were bored at regular intervals through the walls at floor level, presumably for drainage during rain. Against the far wall were stacks of crates being used as hen houses. Climbing those crates and jumping the wall seemed to be my only option. But, before I could get up the crates, I was tackled by the baker, sending us both crashing into the makeshift hen houses.

The baker and I soon found ourselves fighting, not each other, but dozens of angry chickens. I blindly reached into my bag hoping to find one of my cans of pepper spray, but instead found the Taser. I figured that would do just as well and pulled it out. I managed to get it out just as a particularly angry-looking hen launched itself at my face. Instinctively, I brought up my hands to protect myself and luckily struck the perturbed pullet with the charged electrodes. The flash of the discharge, along with the sound the chicken made as it passed out, scared the baker half to death and he beat a hasty retreat back down the stairs.

As soon as he was gone, I turned to try and climb over the wall again. The chickens seemed to rally around their fallen comrade and attacked me again. The Taser made short work of the entire brood and the smell of burnt feathers and chicken poop soon filled the air. After zapping the last chicken and tossing it off the roof, I once again started to climb over the wall. When I was able to see over the wall, my heart sank. The mob had grown even more and, drawn by the screams of the baker, had surrounded the bakery. Several of my pursuers were standing in a circle examining the stunned chicken I had flung over the side. Someone in the crowd saw me, pointed, and started yelling, drawing the attention of everyone else.

I turned away from the wall and jumped down off the crates I had been standing on thinking I needed to find another way down. As soon as I landed, another way presented itself as the floor gave way beneath my feet. I fell through the floor and landed back in the kitchen by the front door, squarely on top of the baker, knocking him out. The two men who were just coming inside to investigate his crazed behavior froze when they saw me, and one of them started to slowly reach for a weapon that was tucked into his belt.

The three of us stood there eying one another for a few moments until a commotion outside drew their attention away from me. The chicken I had Tased and tossed off the roof had regained consciousness and had gone berserk. Some people thought it was a sign, while others thought it was possessed. Either way, it gave me just enough time to run back through the bakery and find the only means of escape I could think of and had purposely overlooked before...the toilet drain.

In the back corner of the building was an angled slab of stone in front of a rectangular hole in the wall. The hole was just big enough for me to slide through with my bag in front of me. The smell inside was even worse than the last one I was in, but that was probably due to the fact that this one was intact.

I slid head first down the chute into the covered ditch that ran underneath the side street. I wiggled and wormed my way through the muck, breathing as little as possible, until I reached the middle of the street where the ditch I was in connected to the one in the middle of the road. Above me I could hear the large mob moving about on the tiles and I hoped they wouldn't think to search the sewers.

When I reached the middle of the road, I was relieved to find that that ditch was slightly wider. The further I traveled through the sewer, the larger it became. Since I was still pushing my bag in front of me, I didn't see the intersection of what had to be the main sewer line until it was too late. Even though the line I was in was big enough to crawl through, I still had to push the bag as far as I could, and then crawl up behind it in order to move through the pipe. When I reached the main line, the bag dropped into the larger ditch and was swept away by the current. Without hesitation I launched myself into the stream and swam after it.

Chapter 26
Finding the Ring

I traveled through the main sewer line for several hundred yards, until it emptied out into a river just outside the city walls. Once free from the pipe, I began to search frantically for my backpack, knowing that I had less than a day before Khan's servant appeared to hide the ring. Twelve and a half hours later the sun was starting to set. I had almost given up hope of finding my bag when I spotted it on the western bank of the river. I swam over to it and quickly took inventory. Satisfied that all was in order, I went to work cleaning everything off and then asked the genie how long I had left to find the ring.

"Sir, I believe you have approximately eighteen hours and twenty-five minutes until the confusion of the languages. Our Mongolian friend should be arriving in about ten hours."

"Alright, that gives me an eight-hour window to find the ring and get out. Wait a sec, what was he doing here for that long? Why didn't he just hide the ring and jump out?"

"When the servant arrived in this time, he appeared very much in the same manner you did. Only when he arrived, or will arrive from your perspective, the people were ready and captured him before he could recover from his disorientation. His captors took him, or will take him, to the bakery you ran through earlier and they accused him of destroying the building. When he denied any involvement in the crime, they locked him in the building next door and confiscated all his belongings with the exception of the ring which he had slipped into his mouth when they started going through his satchel."

I scratched my head for a moment. Something just didn't

seem right about what the genie had said, and then it dawned on me. "If he was locked up, how was he able to hide the ring before the Great Confusion?"

The genie was silent for a moment as if reluctant to answer. When he did answer, it sent chills down my spine. "You will have to let him out, Sir."

"So that's why you said it would be beneficial for me to come back here. Wait a sec, the people were ready because I had appeared first, right? If I hadn't come back he wouldn't have been captured. So why did you suggest that we come here in the first place?" I started to rub my forehead in the spot that only bothered me when contemplating temporal paradoxes.

"The servant would not have been caught if you had not jumped back here. I merely suggested coming back because you would never have been able to dig out the ring from under the ruins of the tower in the present."

"Alright, now that I have changed the past, how do I make sure that he can find his satchel and get himself home?"

"Shortly after the servant hid the ring, the tower was struck and the languages were scrambled. When nobody was able to communicate with anyone other than immediate family, they all packed up and left the city. The city became a ghost town almost overnight. The servant will eventually find his satchel in an abandoned house on the north side of the city, most likely belonging to one of the men who will capture him in the first place."

Letting the matter drop, I decided that I should find a good spot to get some rest and wait. Judging by the tower in the distance, I was on the south side of the city and a little over a mile from where I started. The sewer had deposited me outside the city wall, so I followed it hoping to find a lesser gate in order to get in unnoticed. I didn't like the idea of passing through that main gate again, but it was a lot more appealing than swimming back in the way I came out.

Soon I found a small door through the wall and quietly slipped through it. I wandered through the streets until I recognized the back of the bakery I had run through earlier. After a few more minutes of searching, I found an empty building with a good view of the street where I could get some much-needed rest. I set the alarm on my watch and quickly dropped off to sleep.

Several hours later I was awakened, not by my watch, but by an angry mob marching down the street. I checked my watch and found that I had slept through the alarm, which meant the mob was more than likely the one that captured the servant. Risking a quick glance out the window, I confirmed my suspicion and easily spotted the small man being roughly dragged down the street, his hands bound tightly in front of him.

The mob stopped at the bakery and grew quiet. The largest man in the group stood in the doorway and gestured to the ruined interior and made a loud announcement that I could not begin to understand. The servant, however, seemed to understand perfectly, and answered back, not in the local language, but in flawless English.

"I had nothing to do with the destruction of this primitive building!!!"

The large man, who was obviously the leader of the mob, seemed to understand what the servant said, but was not very pleased about it. He then said something to the men holding the servant and pointed to the building next door. One of the men relieved the servant of his satchel which was tied around his waist. I watched as they started to drag him into the next building and caught a glimpse of the servant slipping something into his mouth before he disappeared inside.

I checked my watch. Six and a half hours until the

confusion. After another thirty minutes or so, the mob dispersed and only one man stayed behind to guard the building where the servant was held. Thinking fast, I pulled the necklace out of my bag and slipped it on. Casually, I stepped out of the building and waved at the guard. He seemed entranced for a moment and then waved back, blushing fiercely. When I motioned with my finger for him to come to me his smile got bigger and after taking a quick look around he started my way. When he was only a few yards away, I cast one last flirtatious glance at the smitten guard and slipped back into the building I had been hiding in. The guard hurried his pace, and just as he came through the door, I stabbed him in the chest with the Taser and dropped him to the floor.

After removing the necklace and checking to see if the street was clear, I dressed in the guard's clothing and made my way to the building where the servant was being held. I tried the door and found it unlocked. The inside of the building had no walls, only wooden beams every few feet with what looked like shackles mounted high up on each side. The servant was blindfolded and shackled to the first beam. He looked as if he had been beaten fairly badly and was barely conscious.

I thought about just taking the ring from him and leaving him there, but then realized that he might not be able to get out at all if I didn't release him, and if he didn't make it back to Khan... I had to stop that train of thought before my head started to hurt.

It only took a few moments to figure out how to free him from the shackles and he slumped down to the floor rubbing his bruised wrists. I started to leave but was stopped by his hand on my leg. I turned to look at him and watched as he pulled the ring out of his mouth and slipped it onto his finger.

"Thank you for releasing me. I don't know who you

are, or why you are helping me, but thank you." His voice
sounded weak and strained. I reached into my pack and
pulled out my canteen. I unscrewed the lid and held the bottle
to his lips. When he had had his fill, I returned it to my bag
and placed a hand on his shoulder.

"My friend, you have had a long, hard journey. You must
finish your mission soon, then you can rest."

The servant nodded and rose to his feet. He set his jaw
with determination and made his way out of the building
without so much as a glance back in my direction. I waited a
few moments, shook my head, and then followed. Once I was
outside it took me a moment to find him again. He wasn't
as frail as I had initially thought. As soon as he had left the
building, he started sprinting toward the tower. I followed as
best I could, pausing only once to slip the necklace back on.
I felt that running through the streets looking like a beautiful
local was better than looking like a guilty stranger.

After making it through the East Gate, the servant
ran, not straight at the tower, but around the southern side,
toward where I had found the carved block in modern times.
I followed him all the way to the southwest corner where
he turned and dove into an open doorway in the base of the
tower. Cautiously, I approached the doorway, half expecting
him to come bursting out again at any moment. Just before I
entered what appeared to be a service tunnel, I stopped and
inspected the lintel. Just as I had hoped, it was the block I had
found with the inscription on it, but without the inscription
yet.

Peering through the doorway and down the long tunnel,
I saw what appeared to be archways into massive storage
rooms. On either side of each arch were brightly lit torches
which filled the room not only with light but also a thick oily
smoke that seemed to cling to the ceiling. Near the far end of
the tunnel, I could just make out a lone figure pass through

one of the arches taking one of the torches with him. The light from his torch seemed to fade away as he walked deeper into the distant room.

I took a quick glance around the outside of the tower and dashed down the tunnel. Just as I was approaching the storage room, I saw the flicker of firelight on the floor signifying the servant's return. I dove to my right through a different archway and hid in the shadows until he passed by.

When I was sure he was gone, I checked my watch, three minutes until the confusion. Not wanting to waste any more time, I dug into my bag and pulled out my flashlight. I sprinted down the tunnel to the room the servant had gone into and played the beam around what I thought was a storage room. It was in fact a crypt. Thousands of shelves lined the walls containing the remains of workers who had died during the construction of the tower. The realization of where I was nearly made me pass out, but the genie's voice brought me back to my senses.

"Sir, the Lord has come to see the city and the confusion is nigh!! We must go now!"

I started to reach for the globe in my bag when a flash of gold on one of the burial shelves caught my attention. There, placed delicately on the finger of one of the deceased, was the ring I was searching for. After confirming with the genie that this was the correct ring, I gently slid it off of the corpse's finger, grabbed the globe and jumped back to my home and my time.

Chapter 27
The Eagle

My first order of business when I recovered from my jump home was to take a nice long shower. As a matter of fact, that was also my second, third, and even fourth order of business. I just couldn't seem to shake the feeling that I was still contaminated with filth from those ancient sewers. When I had scrubbed every inch of my body raw, I went to my desk and pulled out all of the pieces.

"Genie, how do we go about reassembling your lamp? Do we just melt down all the pieces and then pour them into a mold? Is there some kind of magic ritual that needs to be preformed?"

The globe vibrated with his reply, "As I have told you before, all you have to do is find someone with the right equipment and know-how. There is no ritual or special incantation. It does not even have to be in the shape of a lamp. Personally, I would prefer something a bit more symbolic of freedom, if that is still your intent, Sir."

"That is still my intent, Genie. As for the shape, only one comes to mind that represents freedom..."

After several hours of research and phone calls, I finally found a goldsmith that would work in the quantities I was going to provide. I was surprised at the difficulty of finding one until I considered that the globe weighed just over fourteen pounds by itself. I carefully placed all the pieces in a briefcase and drove out to the goldsmith's place of business.

The whole procedure took five days to complete. First, we had to draw up what I wanted the final shape to be. Then the goldsmith had make the cast for it. He started to complain when I told him that the gold had to be as pure when he was finished as when he had started, which meant he couldn't add any alloys or fillers to the mix. His complaining stopped abruptly when I told him that I would pay him three times his initial estimate if he was able to finish the piece to my specifications. On the fifth day, he called me back to his office to pick up the completed piece.

"Mr. Jonson, I will say that this has been one of the most challenging projects I have ever undertaken. The sheer amount of gold used in this one piece is staggering. The combined weight of the piece is just under thirty-five troy pounds or, if you prefer, just over four hundred and nineteen troy ounces, which at today's gold prices is worth $257,516.07...a very expensive statue, if I do say so myself."

I opened up the case that was sitting on his desk and nodded appreciatively. This man had been true to his word and made a beautiful piece of art. There, nested in a protective cushion of red velvet, was a very lifelike statue of a bald eagle. Of course, I would have to wait until I got home to see if the procedure had worked as far as the genie was concerned. Carefully, I closed the lid on the case, and true to my word as he was to his, I handed over a check worth three times his estimate. With a spring in my step and a smile on my face, I walked back out to my car to drive home.

Just before pulling out of the parking lot, I lifted the lid on the case to try and satisfy my curiosity.

"Genie? Did it work? Are you whole?"

For a long moment I was answered with silence, then gently the voice of the genie filled the car, "Yes, I am here. We were successful."

The eagle statue slowly lifted out of the case and drifted into the back seat. With a flash, the eagle disappeared and in its place was a man dressed in a formal suit, complete with tails, white gloves, and a bow tie. His white hair was slicked back, and his piercing eyes spoke of eons of experiences. He had the air of a man who had been in the service of others his whole life and his voice seemed to have taken on a slight British accent.

I sat there taking in his appearance before speaking. "You don't look at all like what I expected."

The genie raise a single eyebrow as if amused. "What did you expect, Sir? Blue skin and an Hawaiian shirt?"

I let out a short laugh. "No, nothing like that. Besides, I don't think I care for monkeys all that much, although a flying carpet might be fun..."

"Well, Sir, now that you have reassembled all of my pieces, and I have regained my powers, what is it that you want most?"

I opened my mouth to answer, but nothing came immediately to mind. "I don't know. I guess I have everything I want that you could give me... The one thing I don't have, your own laws prevent you from providing." I started the car and pulled out of the parking lot. "Of course if you could make someone fall in love with me, I could never be certain it was real."

The genie nodded knowingly, "You are, of course, referring to the former Miss Maryweather, Mrs. Susan Blackwell. She is where she is meant to be."

We rode in silence the rest of the way home. As we pulled into the driveway an idea occurred to me. The genie might not be able to help my with my love life, but he could help me figure out a mystery that had been nagging at me since basic training graduation day.

"Genie, can you change my physical appearance?"

"How so, Sir?"

"I have been trying to figure out what happened to one of the trainees in my basic training unit for quite some time now. Since you have all of your powers, I was wondering if you could change my appearance, give me a new identity, and send me back to my basic training unit so I can find out what happened to that individual. Heck, make me stronger, faster, and smarter than anyone in my unit, forge the paperwork to get me into my old platoon, and I'll go through basic all over again!"

"Um, Sir, if you told me the name of the trainee in question, I could just tell you what became of him."

"No, no, no. I have made up my mind. Genie, improve me, disguise me, and send me back. At the end of graduation, meet me by the PX to bring me back home."

"As you wish, Sir. I will make it appear as if you are a late arrival. You can meet up with your platoon at basic clothing issue."

Before I knew what was happening, I found myself standing on Fort Jackson just outside the building where we were issued our initial gear. I looked down at myself and was pleasantly surprised with what the genie had done to my body. Where there had once been a wiry young man in his early thirties, now stood a twenty-something gentleman with the body of a Nordic god. I looked around for some kind of reflective surface to see how my face had been changed. Before I could find any kind of suitable mirror, I was approached by a Drill Sergeant from the reception battalion.

"RECRUIT! What are you doing wandering around out here by yourself?!?"

I immediately snapped to parade rest. "Drill Sergeant, I was late getting here and I was instructed to meet my company at basic clothing and issue. I'm not exactly sure where that is."

The training NCO eyed me suspiciously for a few seconds and held out his hand. "Give me your paperwork, recruit."

I was caught off guard by his request until I realized that

I was holding a manila envelope in my left hand. I handed over what I assumed to be my military records. Thinking back to my first time through, I vaguely remembered carrying something similar during reception. As the drill sergeant started leafing through the bundle of papers, I realized that I didn't even know the name that the genie had given me.

After finding the information he was seeking, the drill sergeant carefully placed all the papers back into the envelope and handed it back to me. He looked me over a couple times as if trying to decide whether or not to smoke me for being out on my own.

Apparently satisfied with my demeanor, the drill sergeant let me off the hook with a wave of his hand. "Come on Private, I'll take you to your unit. And Jameson, next time you are ordered to be somewhere, make sure you're on time."

When everyone was dismissed from graduation, I made a beeline for the PX. The last nine weeks of basic training had been a blast and had answered so many questions that had arisen the first time through. It was almost a shame when it was over, but I was ready to go home. Besides, I had one more promise to fulfill.

The only person standing outside the PX entrance was an older gentleman in an officer's dress blue uniform. The rank on his shoulders denoted a three-star general, and the salad on his chest showed that he was well seasoned. However, one look at his face and I knew it was all a ruse. It was, in fact, the genie in disguise. Still, in order to keep up appearances, I walked up to him, saluted, and stood at attention as if awaiting orders.

The genie shook his head before asking, "Did you find out all you wanted to know, Sir?"

"Yeah, and I believe in this situation, given the rank on your collar, I should be calling *you* Sir. As for finding my answers, you could have just told me what had become of Jameson... But, then 'Jameson' wouldn't have existed at all, would he?"

"That is correct, Sir. Are you ready to go home?"

"The sooner the better. And if you could change me back to my former self, I would be very appreciative."

"As you wish."

Half a heartbeat later we were standing in the office of my house and I was back in my old body again. I took a deep breath and then turned to the genie.

"Well, I guess there is only one thing left to do. Genie, I wish for your freedom."

As soon as the words left my lips there was a tremendous clap of thunder and a bright flash that filled the room. When my vision cleared, the genie was still standing before me, only now he was holding the eagle statue. That, and a large smile had spread across his face.

"You're still here? I thought you would have disappeared when I granted you your freedom."

"Sir, if that is what you would like me to do, I will. However, several years ago you told me to 'stick around' once I had been freed in order to keep you sane. Since I am forever in your debt for releasing me, I humbly offer my services for as long as you require them."

"What kind of services? Like a butler or something?"

The genie nodded, "I could be a butler, or a cook, or anything else you require."

I liked the idea of having a butler, especially with this huge house that needed to be cleaned every now and then. There was just one snag...

"I can't very well keep calling you Genie any more if you are going to be my butler... How about... Gene? No, that doesn't suit you..." I snapped my fingers, "I got it. What do you think about the name Martin? Yeah, that suits you.

Martin... Smith. What do you think?"

"I believe that will do nicely, Sir."

"Martin, I believe this is the beginning of a beautiful friendship."

Epilogue

Martin saved his progress and printed off two copies of the memoirs. With a flash he delivered one of them directly to the publishing firm as Mr. Jonson had requested. He stood up from the desk and walked over to the safe behind the row of books on the shelf. He deftly spun the combination on the dial, opened the safe, and gently removed the contents. The picture of Susan and the other copy of the memoirs went into an envelope along with a notice that she and her grandchildren should be present for the reading of Mr. Jonson's last will and testament. According to the will, everything, with the exception of the eagle statue and his bank accounts, was to be split among her grandchildren. The statue was to remain in the possession of Martin Smith and the accounts were to be signed over to Susan and her husband, James.

After one last walk through the house, Martin picked up his statue off the desk and looked down at a picture he had given his friend for his seventy-fifth birthday. It was a picture of the two of them standing next to the hole in the wall where the Camaro had just been removed. The inscription on the frame read "It can't be that bad, can it?"

Martin reached out and touched the image of his friend and said aloud, "I will see you soon, my friend."

And with a flash, Martin was gone.

THE END

Appendix 1
The Life (and Times) of David

(#) **= Denotes Time jump order**
Normal time
Time travel to get the necklace
Time travel to get rich
Time travel to retrieve the globe after it was stolen
Time travel to retrieve the dragon piece
<u>Time travel to retrieve the Buddha piece</u>
<u>Time travel to retrieve the ring</u>

<u>7</u>	*<u>10/23/2242 BC, 0100 hrs</u>*	*<u>Arrives in Shinar/Babel to retrieve the ring</u>*
<u>6</u>	<u>4/13/1883, 0130 hrs</u>	**<u>Arrive in Bohd Gaya to retrieve the Buddha</u>**
5	*1/1/1916, 0100 hrs*	***Arrives in the Forbidden City to retrieve the dragon piece***
	1/2/1916	***Returns to 9/21/2006***
1	7/6/1940, 0800 hrs	**Arrives (twice) to retrieve the necklace**
	6/30/1980	Birth
2	<u>5/23/1991, 1815 hrs</u>	<u>Arrives on runway of Flying Dollar Airport, causes crash, robs self</u>
	<u>5/24/1991, 0015 hrs</u>	<u>Goes forward to 6/11/2001 to cash bonds (3)</u>
4	4/10/1996	<u>Arrives to sell gold, hires investment secretary. Globe stolen!</u> *Arrives from Gomez Plant to get the globe, returns to Gomez Plant to return the "borrowed" globe.*
	<u>10/24/1996</u>	<u>Builds dream house</u>
	<u>6/30/1998</u>	<u>Buys Camaro</u>
	5/21/2001	Camaro crash <u>(secretary and her boyfriend)</u>
	<u>6/4/2001</u>	<u>Transfer all money to an off shore account. Come under investigation for insider trading.</u>
<u>3</u>	<u>6/11/2001</u>	Arrives to cash bonds, causes Gomez Chicken Plant destruction <u>After cashing bonds, buys gold.</u> *During chicken plant destruction, the third David steals the globe to retrieve his own and then returns to 8/27/2006.*

<u>6/11/2001</u>	<u>Jumps back to 4/10/1996 (4)</u>
8/8/2001	Begins basic training
3/14/2002	Graduates from AIT
6/5/2005	Hummer accident
6/7/2005	Deployed to Iraq
10/27/2005	Aircraft damaged
11/17/2005	Hanger door incident
3/14/2006	FOUND GLOBE
6/6/2006	Returns stateside
7/8/2006	**Jumps back to retrieve necklace (1)**
8/28/2006	Leaves service, time paradox, <u>travels back to 5/23/1991 (2) to get rich</u>
9/4/2006	Buys mansion in Simpsonville, South Carolina (where he lives present day)
9/18/2006	Departs for Beijing in search of the dragon piece
9/20/2006	Visits Forbidden City in search of the dragon piece
9/21/2006	***Jumps to 1/1/1916 (5) to retrieve the dragon piece***
10/14/2006	Susan and James get married
<u>10/21/2006</u>	**<u>Jumps to 4/13/1883, 0130 hrs (6) to retrieve Buddha piece</u>**
<u>10/25/2006</u>	***<u>Jumps to 10/23/2242 BC, 0100 hrs (7) to retrieve the ring</u>***
10/27/2006	Takes ALL pieces to goldsmith
11/01/2006	Picks up eagle and makes a wish to find out what happened to Jameson
1/15/2060	Begins memoirs
5/25/2060	First doctor's appointment
5/28/2060	Test results
8/25/2060	Death of David
8/26/2060	Memoirs finished by Martin

Appendix 2
References

1. On page 9, Private Leonard Lawrence was a character in the movie *Full Metal Jacket* (1987) and was played by Vincent D'Onofrio.

2. On page 13, Private Cameron uses the phrase "Show me the money" to accept a dare. This is a quote from the movie *Jerry Maguire* (1996).

3. On page 31, David's description of the march home as "slow, weary, depressing yet determined walk of men who have nothing left in life except the impulse to simply sol–" is a direct quote from the movie *A Knight's Tale* (2001) by the character Geoffrey Chaucer, who was played by Paul Bettany, when he was giving the definition of "to trudge."

4. On page 51, the young TV doctor that was vaguely referred to was Dr. Doogie Howser, played by Neil Patrick Harris, from the show *Doogie Howser, MD* (1989 - 1993)

5. On page 79, when the genie gives fire to Adam and Eve, he declares his name to be Prometheus. This, of course, is a direct reference to the Greek myth of Prometheus who is said to have stolen fire from the gods and given it to man, only to be punished by the gods by being chained to a rock to have his liver pecked out by vultures. I realize, by the way, that this scenario is not Biblically accurate. Angels who disagree with God are fallen angels in reality, but this is fiction.

6. On page 81, many of the details about Genghis Khan were collected from Wikipedia.

7. On Page 109, I used an actual plane "incident" that is documented on the NTSB website. Flying Dollar Airport, May 23, 1991.

8. On page 152, the argument between Martin and David was a very close, but not exact, quote from the movie *Star Trek VI: The Undiscovered Country* (1991) in the scene where the Klingon and Enterprises command staff are having dinner together.

9. The dream sequence on page 154 is making fun of the movie *Final Destination* (2000).

10. On page 158, the information about the Taihe Dian, or Hall of Supreme Harmony, comes from the website www. kinabaloo.com/fch.html.

11. On page159, the story about Yuan Shikai is true, at least according to Wikipedia.

12. The description of Sir Alexander Cunningham on page 190 came from a picture found online at http://dictionary. buddhistdoor.com/en/word/107768/sir%20alexander%20 cunningham.

13. On page 209, relative to the location of the Tower of Babel, see www.answersingenesis.org/articles/arj/v4/ n1/where-is-tower-babel. It is said to be in Northeastern Syria in the Upper Khabur River triangle, not far from Tell Brak.